KB274809

숭실대학교 한국문예연구소 문예총서 13

SONGS FROM KOREA

변영태가 쓴 영시집

한국의 詩歌

민충환 편

지식과교양

부천은 변영로를 낳은 시인의 고향이다. 그간 수주(樹州)의 자료를 찾고 주해서(註解書)와 시 전집 등을 만드는 일에 온 힘을 다 기울였다. 그에 대한 정리가 얼추 마무리되었다고 믿어 내친김에 그의 형제에 대한 연구로 확대시켰다.

잘 알려진 바와 같이 중국 당나라 때 문장가 삼소(三蘇 : 소순, 소철, 소식)를 본떠 주변 사람들은 변영로 삼형제를 일러 '삼변(三卞)'이라 했다.

장남 변영만은 법조인이자 한학자였고, 둘째 변영태는 외무부장관과 국무총리를 지낸 정치가였고, 셋째 변영로는 시인이자 교육자였다.

변영만 전집은 기출판되었으니 자연히 관심은 일석(逸石) 변영태에게로 향했다. 그가 남긴 저술로는 〈나의 조국〉(1956), 〈외교어록〉(1959) 등이 있는데 특히 내 눈을 끈 것은 영시집(英詩集) 〈Songs From Korea〉(국제문화협회, 1948)이었다. 이 책은 우리 고시조 102수를 영역한 것과 자작 영시 32편 그리고 부록으로 고시조 작가의 약력을 덧붙이고 있다.

우리 문학 작품을 외국어로 번역하여 세계로 널리 알려야 한다는 목소리가 점차 높아가고 있는 이때에 일석의 이러한 선구적 업적은 새롭게 조명해야 할 주요 문학연구 자료라 할 수 있다. 또한 일석은 정치가로만 인식되었는데 여기에 실린 영시를 통해 뛰어난 시인으로,

번역문학가로 재평가되어야 한다. 그의 시는 매우 아름다울 뿐만 아니라 기독교 문학의 지평을 넓힌 성과로 기록될 만하기 때문이다.

이 작업을 하면서 땅 속에 묻혀있던 문화재를 발굴하여 세상에 드러낸 것 같은 큰 기쁨을 느꼈다.

이 책을 내는 데에 많은 분들의 정성어린 도움이 있었다. 부천문화원은 귀한 자료를 제공해 주었고, 구정혜·고정임 문우와 제자 김선미 양은 워드 작업을 해주었으며, 서문(序文)은 김영배 선생이 2부 자작 영시와 부록은 우형숙 박사가 각각 우리말로 번역해 주었고, 1부의 시조 원문을 규명하는 데에는 김학성 교수가 친절히 자문해 주었다. 그리고 조규익 교수의 각별한 관심과 후의에 힘입어 이 책이 출간될 수 있었다.

끝으로, 본서 발간에 밀양 변씨 종친회의 후원이 있었음을 밝히며 많은 분들께 깊이 감사드린다.

2011년 9월

편자 씀

CONTENTS

목 차

"Si-jo" is the time-honoured form of poetry in pure Korean tongue, distinct from those of Chinese poems. It has almost all the regularity of the English sonnet, only shorter by half. It has its own pauses, too, in spite of its shortness. It is essentially a thing to be sung, and has often been improvised on occasions of rejoicings. There is no dating it back exactly, but it would be quite safe to say that this sole form of vernacular versification has been in constant use for these 800 years. If one swallow is allowed to make the summer, its history extends further back. As all such simple things should, it must be lucid, direct, single in point, and yet it must not be one trailing sentence with no pause, plausibly chopped into lines.

Rightly or wrongly, none of our poets has ever made a serious business of poetry to the degree that Wordsworth did, far less in expressing themselves with "si-jo". If they wrote poetry at all, they did so not merely because they had something to say, but also because they could say it lightly and playfully. This throws light on the fact that neither fierce preaching nor deep philosophy is to be found in their lines of verse. It is not that they were incapable of sustained thought but that they would have sooner put down serious ideas in anything else but poetry. You will find that some of the songs here given are somewhat out of keeping with the general delineations of their authors' characters. That simply means that they were off guard, not self-conscious, and then that often they did not mean all they said.

In the interpretation of a "si-jo", much depends upon how you make out the meaning of the term "nim" which frequently occurs. The presence of this peculiar word necessarily makes the poem look like a love ditty. But it is as often not as it is. The word means "the one to whom I am devoted", or more exactly, "the one who possesses me." In many cases, it signifies the king or any other object of devotion. In the translations, an attempt has been made to remove the confusion.

Many of the songs are pervaded with a love of Nature, perhaps of a most sane sort, never so deep as to be akin to worship, neither morbid in any manner, but just enough to render life tolerable — in a word, a chummy sort of love, never tired, never surfeited. It is quite a something to start with and, if need be, to fall back upon.

Confucius briefly criticizes the three hundred poems of the ancients he collected in a book by calling them innocent. With much more truth, he would have said the same of these songs. If some of them be found to be dogs, then they will also be found barking. Nobody is expected to be harmed by them. More likely than not they will help us along our path not exactly by affording us strength but perhaps by airing what mischievously lurks within us lightly and humorously.

It is with most of these Korean songs as with short poems in general—much of the beauty lies in their music of words reducible to sound, not in the subject matter, that is, not so much in the things they say as in how they read orally. The former can be easily transplanted in another language, but, as to the latter, nothing definite can be said. If you succeed in conveying the music, the magic, too, then you are fortunate, a thing to be thankful for, not to be proud of. If you fail, you have done what was reasonably expected to be done, no worse. This amounts to admitting that poetry is not amenable to translation. Strictly speaking, yes. But impossibilities are always aimed at, strived for. And why not this particular one? What is the use of our being furnished with a better brain after all? No, no, it would not do to waive this human prerogative. We must go on torturing poems, and. when what is elusive eludes, leaving something imbecile, we are not to despair but to make the best of the situation by imagining ourselves into the bliss that would be ours if what has apparently eluded had not.

No apologies should be sufficient for the bad form I commit by introducing some of my own English poems mostly written in my youth. The enormity is all the more flagrant, considering that the translations are all works of people long dead, and that from them alone the title of the book is assumed. The only feature that ought to contribute toward homogeneity, however, is that they all have the common medium of English and that, things of my own writing as they are, they are as dead to me now as the ancients'. You will have understood me to surmise that I felt called, in a manner nobody knows, to give them some sort of light, and, failing to afford a separate appearance, had to arrange for them to accompany their venerable companions.

Those songs whose authors are known are arranged either in the order of their birth dates or, where they can not be ascertained, according to the order of the kings whom they are known to have served. Then follow the anonymous poems in no sort of arrangement at all. They just jostle along as we do. All of the old songs have no themes. Indeed, their being so short might constitute an adequate excuse for having none at all. In a sense, they are themes themselves. However, they look like one another as so many prison inmates so that they are as conveniently numbered.

To allow the songs to speak for themselves and let nothing interrupt their reading, the biographical notes are attached at the end of the book in the alphabetical order. But interest is hoped to be added thereby and much light thrown on the interpretation of the songs themselves.

Many thanks are due to Mr. I-byung-geui of the Hwi-moon Middle School, who has so generously placed his rare information on folk-songs at my disposal and made it possible to clear numerous doubts about the original text, authorship and other important points. And also I cannot appreciate enough the painstaking perusal of the manuscript and valuable suggestions of Miss D. R. Jones, my comrade in the English-teaching crusade.

1948. Y. T. Pyun

서문(序文)

　　시조(時調)는 중국의 시와는 구별되는 오랜 전통을 가진 한국 고유의 시가 형식이다. 시조는 영시의 소네트와 거의 유사한 규칙성을 가지고 있는데 차이점이라면 시가의 구절이 소네트의 반 정도라는 뿐이며 또한 그 짧은 형식에도 불구하고 고유의 구절도 가지고 있다. 시조는 운율이 그 필수적 요소이기도 하며 여러 흥겨운 모임에서 즉흥적으로 창작되기도 했다. 시조의 연원(淵源)에 대한 정확한 기록은 없지만 그 고유의 시가 형태는 800여 년 동안 꾸준히 이어져 왔다. 약간의 추측성 속단을 해본다면 그 기원은 좀 더 이른 시대로 거슬러 올라갈 수도 있다. 거의 모든 단시(短時) 종류들이 그렇듯이 시조도 그 형태에 있어서 간단명료하며 또한 지루하게 한 문장으로 길게 늘어지지 않고 적절한 구절로 단락 지어진다.

　　다소 이견은 있겠지만, 시조 작가들은 윌리엄 워즈워드처럼 작시(作詩)를 심오한 업으로 삼는 사람들이 거의 없으며 시조라는 형식으로 흉중(胸中)을 털어놓는다는 점에서 더더욱 그러하다. 시조작가들은 그저 무언가 할 말이 있어서 썼고 또한 흥겨운 유희의 일환으로 그것을 불렀으며 이 점이 바로 시조의 시구(詩句)에 어떤 근엄한 교훈이나 깊은 철학이 내포되지 않음을 명약관화(明若觀火)하게 보여준다. 그 이유는 시조작가들이 확고한 사상을 가지고 있지 못해서가 아니라 그들이 적어도 시조에서 만큼은 심오한 사상을 심기 싫어서였을 것이다. 독자들은 이 책에 실려 있는 시조들을 보며 그 내용이 작가의 인물 정보와는 사뭇 다른 점들을 보게 될 것이다. 그것은 작가들이 한가한 여가시간에 별 거리낌없이 일종의 유희거리로 시를 썼다는 것을 의미한다.

시조를 해석함에 있어 '님'이라는 단어가 종종 등장하는데 이 단어는 많은 뜻을 함축하고 있어 그 뜻을 해석하는 데 매우 다양한 유추가 필요하다. 이 독특한 단어의 존재는 시조를 일견(一見) 사랑의 소곡(小曲)처럼 보이게 하는데 실상은 그렇지 않은 경우가 많다. 그 단어는 종종 '내가 헌신(獻身)하는 사람' 좀 더 정확히는 '나를 소유하고 있는 사람'을 의미한다. 이 단어는 왕 또는 다른 헌신의 주체를 상징하는 경우도 또한 많다. 번역에 있어서 이 단어의 혼돈을 없애기 위한 많은 노력을 기울였다.

많은 시조들이 자연에 대한 사랑을 주제로 창작되었는데, 그것은 신앙적인 숭배의 모습이라기보다는 건전한 자연예찬 종류들이며 그 표현방식도 복잡다단(複雜多端)하거나 과장된 형식이 아닌 평이하며 사랑 어린 것들이 대부분이다. 이러한 자연예찬의 형식은 새로이 시작된 것이며 필요에 따라 편안함을 주는 역할도 한다.

일찍이 중국의 성현 공자는 그가 수집 편찬한 고전 '시경(詩經)'의 시 삼백 편을 일컬어 "詩 三百 一言以蔽之 曰 思無邪"라 간략히 평했다. 아마 그가 시조를 감상할 수 있었더라면 틀림없이 위와 같은 표현을 썼을 것이다. 간혹 졸렬(拙劣)한 시조도 있을 수 있겠지만 누구도 그로 인해 해를 입진 않을 것이다. 그것들은 우리에게 직접적인 힘을 부여하기 보다는 오히려 우리 내부의 장난기 어린 잠재적인 힘을 가볍고 유머러스한 방식으로 구현시키어 올바른 길로 나아가도록 유도한다.

이 책에 실린 시조의 대부분은 간결하다. 또한 그 아름다움은 거창한 주제가 아니라 소리로 표현될 수 있는 성조(聲調)에 있는데 그것은 그 아름다움이 말하는 것에 있다는 것이 아니라 입을 통하여 발음되어지는 성조에 있다는 것을 의미한다. 번역함에 있어 전자의 경우는 다른 언어로의 변환작업이 비교적 쉽게 이루어지는 반면 후자의 경우는 그리 녹록치 않다. 만약 당신이 음악이나 마술(魔術)을 다른 언어로 번역하는 데 성공했다면 그것은 행운이며 감사해야 할 일이지 널리 자랑할 거리는 못되며 마찬가지로 당신이 실패했더라도 그것은 흔히 일어날 일이 일어난 것일 뿐 그리 나쁜 것은 아니다. 이 점은 바로 시조를 번역하기가 힘들다는 것임을 의미한다. 엄밀히 말해서 그렇다. 하지만 불가능이란 항상 목표로 설정하여 투쟁하는 대상일진대, 시조라고 거기서 예외가 될 순 없지 않은가? 이 좋은 머리를 그저 방치할 것인가? 아니다, 그건 아니다. 인간으로서 가진 이 특권을 포기해선 안된다. 우리는 시의 이해에 대한 노력을 꾸준히 하여야 하며 뜻이 교묘하여 이해하기 난해한 작품이어서 비록 그 일부를 포기할지언정 가능한 모든 상상의 나래를 펼쳐 시의 세계라는 축복의 땅으로 진입하는 노력을 꾸준히 하여야 한다.

내가 젊은 시절에 쓴 대부분의 영시들의 조악(粗惡)한 형태들은 여기서 아무리 사죄해본들 그저 더욱 더 부끄러울 따름이다. 그 번역물들이 오래 전 작고한 작가들의 것임과 그 책의 제목 또한 그들에게서 취한 것에 이르면 그 송구스러움은 극에 달한다 하겠다. 그 작품들이 가진 유일한 동질적인 특징은 영어라는 매개 언어로 쓰였다는 것과 비록 내가 쓴 글이긴 하지만 지금은 마치 고전작가의 글처럼 죽은 듯 보인다는 점이다.

이 책의 수록작품들은 작가가 밝혀진 작품들의 경우는 생년월일 순으로, 출생 연도가 확실치 않은 경우엔 그 작가가 살았던 시대의 왕계(王系)의 순서에 따랐다. 무명씨(無名氏)의 작품은 별다른 수록방침 없이 필자와 출판사가 임의로 선택한 순서대로 수록했다. 모든 작품은 주제가 없는데 시조의 간결함이 그에 대한 적절한 해명이 될 듯도 하다. 어느 의미에선 수록작품 그 하나하나가 주제 그 자체로 봐도 무방할 것이다. 또한 이 작품들은 서로가 마치 교도소 내의 많은 수인(囚人)과 비슷하게 각자 알맞게 번호로 매겨졌다. 작가들의 약력은 작품들을 스스로 낭송하고 읽는 데 방해가 되지 않도록 배려하여 책의 말미(末尾)에 알파벳 순으로 수록하였다. 비록 약력을 뒷부분에 수록하였지만 그것이 작품자체의 이해를 돕는 데 일조(一助)할 것이라 믿어 의심치 않는다.

이 책을 출판하는 데 있어 원문, 원작자 등 여러 주요한 문제들에 대한 필자의 의문점을 해소할 수 있도록 고전시가에 관한 희귀자료를 아낌없이 제공해 주신 휘문중학교의 이병기(李秉岐) 선생께 무한한 감사의 말을 드린다. 또한 수고를 마다않고 원고를 정독하며 소중한 제언(提言)을 해주신 나의 영어교육 십자군 동료인 D. R. Jones 양께도 감사의 말을 전한다.

1948. 변영태

PART 1
TRANSLATIONS OF
OLD KOREAN SONGS

_시조번역

1

One holding thorns to block the way

Age would come by, the other hand

Twirling a big club to dismay

The Hoary Hair, I made a stand.

But vain ! For he this plan did see

And by a short cut stole on me.

Oo-tag[1]

한 손에 가시를 들고 또 한 손에 막대 들고

늙는 길 가시로 막고 오는 백발 막대로 치렸더니

백발이 제 먼저 알고 지름길로 오더라. [2]

우탁(禹倬)

---

1 성명 표기 방법은 오늘과 다르지만 여기서는 당시의 시대적 배경을 감안, 원문 그대로 하였다.
2 본서에서 시조 원문은 심재완, 「정본 시조대전」(일조각, 1984)의 '현철(現綴)' 내용을 따랐다.

2

E'en if I die again, again,

To hundred and first death, my shape

A handful o' dust in earth remain,

And all ideas dissolved escape,

This single heart for him, my King,

Shall know no change through aeons' ring.

Jung-mong-joo

이 몸이 죽어 죽어 일백 번 고쳐 죽어

백골이 진토(塵土) 되어 넋이라도 있고 없고

님 향한 일편단심(一片丹心)이야 가실 줄이 있으랴.

정몽주(鄭夢周)

3

Immaculate egret, do not go

To the vale where dark-hued crows fight

With one another, for, you know,

Enraged crows they envy white,

Be in wise fear and strive to save

What is made clean by ocean's wave.

Jung-mong-joo's mother

까마귀 싸우는 골에 백로야 가지 마라

성낸 까마귀 흰빛을 새올세라

청강(淸江)에 좋이 씻은 몸을 더러일까 하노라.

정몽주 모친(母親)

4

Ah! we are all in Destiny's hand.

The Full Moon Terrace lies in weed,

Where kings five centuries ruled the land,

All left to the shepherd's pipe of reed.

The sun sets o'er the empty height,

And, why, tears blur this passer's sight!

Wun-chun-sug

흥망이 유수(有數)하니 만월대(滿月臺)도 추초(秋草)로다

오백 년 왕업(王業)이 목적(牧笛)에 부쳤으니

석양에 지는 객이 눈물겨워 하노라.

원천석(元天錫)

 5

Though pleasant to you, never do

What others find the opposite,

Nor an unjust thing, even though

It be at popularity's height.

Let us so live as to ensure

Keeping our nature free and pure.

Byun-gye-ryang

내해 좋다 하고 남 싫은 일 하지 말며

남이 한다 하고 의(義) 아니면 좇지 말리

우리는 천성(天性)을 지키어 삼긴 대로 하리라.

변계량(卞季良)[1]

---

1 앞의 책에는 주의식(朱義植) 작으로 되어 있음.

6

The seat of half-millenial reign

I reach, a lone man on a bay;

The landscapes, as of old, remain,

But where are those who held the sway?

Ah! the good old days must have been

A short-lived, vanishing dream-scene!

Gil-jai

오백년 도읍지를 필마(匹馬)로 돌아드니

산천은 의구(依舊)하되 인걸(人傑)은 간 데 없다

어즈버 태평연월(太平烟月)이 꿈이런가 하노라.

길재(吉再)

7

I know what I should like to be

When this life's journey I am through;

Were freedom to be left to me,

A pine with many a sweeping bough,

On th' highest peak, I would be and

Alone green in a snow-bound land.

Sung-sam-moon

이 몸이 죽어 가서 무엇이 될꼬 하니

봉래산 제일봉에 낙락장송(落落長松) 되어 있어

백설이 만건곤(滿乾坤)할 제 독야청청(獨也靑靑)하리라.

성삼문(成三問)

8

The north wind whistles in the trees;

The moon is cold o'er th' snowy town.

At a border post where ice e'er is,

I, leaning on my sword undrawn,

Stand with triumphant manful cry;

Before me nations conquered lie.

Gim-jong-su

삭풍(朔風)은 나무 끝에 불고 명월은 눈 속에 찬데

만리변성(萬里邊城)에 일장검(一長劍) 짚고 서서

긴 파람 큰 한 소리에 거칠 것이 없어라.

김종서(金宗瑞)

9

Night falls o'er the autumnal stream;

The waves are stilled; I lay the hook

Beneath the surface that does gleam,

But no bite, nor a bright outlook.

Homeward the empty boat I row,

Only laden with serene moon's glow.

Wul-san-dai-goon

추강(秋江)에 밤이 드니 물결이 차노매라

낚시 드리치니 고기 아니 무노매라

무심한 달빛만 싣고 빈 배 저어 오노매라.

월산대군(月山大君)

10

I forget what I hear at once

And pretend not to see what's seen.

My principle is to be a dunce :

On neighbours' right-wrongs I'm not keen.

My hand is still good as of old

And it shall only goblets hold.

Song-soon

들은 말 즉시 잊고 본 일도 못 본 듯이

내 인사 이러하매 남의 시비 모를로다

다만 지 손이 성하니 잔 잡기만 하노라.

송순(宋純)[1]

---

1 앞의 책에는 송인(宋寅 ; 1516~1584) 작으로 되어 있음.

11

Lad, you needn't bother 'bout the mat;

These fallen leaves suit me so well.

Neither ignite the light-wood fat;

The moon is up that last night fell.

Only mind not to grudge the wine,

Whether it's out of taste or fine.

Han-hwag[1]

짚방석 내지 마라 낙엽엔들 못 앉으랴

솔불 혀지 마라 어제 진 달 돋아온다

아이야 박주산챌(薄酒山菜)망정 없다 말고 내어라.

한호(韓濩)

---

1 한자 '濩'는 퍼질·풍류 호, 기슭 물 떨어질 확, 두 가지로 읽히는데 본서의 지은이는 '확'
으로 읽음. 여기서는 '한호'로 바로 잡았다.

12

Who can it be you've parted from,

O Candle in the draughty cot,

That you weep in that rueful form,

Yet that your heart burns know it not?

Ah! you, too, like me, never find

How it's consumed and undermined.

I-gai

방안에 혔는 촉(燭)불 눌과 이별하였건대

겉으로 눈물지고 속 타는 줄 모르는고

우리도 저 촉불 같아야 속 타는 줄 모르노라.

이개(李塏)

13

The shallow wailed throughout the night

As the stream fretted o'er the stones.

I couldn't forbear, try as I might,

Taking it for your bitter moans

Of woe. O could itbackward flow

And how I weep, too, let you know.

Wun-ho

간밤에 울던 여울 슬피 울어 지내어다

이제야 생각하니 님이 울어 보내도다

저 물이 거슬리 흐르고자 나도 울어 녜리라.

원호(元昊)

14

My mind befooled so utterly,

All that I do is of a dunce;

How can my love here near me be,

Beyond the dim hills for the nonce;

Yet, as leaves wind-spun crisply leap,

I listen for his steps and peep.

Su-gyung-dug

마음이 어린 후니 하는 일이 다 어리다
만중운산(萬重雲山)에 어느 님 오리마는
지는 잎 부는 바람에 행여 귄가 하노라.

서경덕(徐敬德)

15

O friend, let that which I am be
And do not wish me otherwise!
Should a clown mar his existence free
With thoughts of making self look nice?
Far less should this incurable child
Of Nature born blind, deaf and wild.

I-hwang

이런들 어떠하며 저런들 어떠하료
초야우생(草野愚生)이 이렇다 어떠하료
하물며 천석고황(泉石膏肓)을 고쳐 무슴하료.

이황(李滉)

16

The fragrant orchids in the dell

I love without quite knowing why;

The fleecy clouds (I cannot tell

How) look so winsome in the sky.

Amid these scenes it's harder yet

The Fairest One all to forget.

I-hwang

유란(幽蘭)이 재곡(在谷)하니 자연이 듣기 좋애

백운(白雲)이 재산(在山)하니 자연이 보기 좋애

이 중에 피미일인(彼美一人)을 더욱 잊지 못하애.

이황(李滉)

17

Before the hill there is a bower;

Below the bower lies the sea.

The gulls in flocks that speak of power

There settle at will and scream in glee.

But lone white Crane, why do you pause

And stand aloof? Tell me the cause.

I-hwang

산전(山前)에 유대(有臺)하고 대하(臺下)에 유수(流水)로다

떼 많은 갈매기는 오명가명하거든

어떻다 교교백구(皎皎白駒)는 멀리 마음하는고.

이황(李滉)

18

Name and career I've thrown away.

What are they now but worn-out shoes?

At my old place I'm back to stay,

Now finding friends in deer and moose.

Maybe my life spent in such state,

Too, is the gift of my Potentate.

I-hwang

당시(當時)에 녀던 길을 몇 해를 버려 두고

어디 가 다니다가 이제사 돌아온고

이제나 돌아오나니 년데 마음 말으리.

이황(李滉)

19

I wonder how the hill remains

Through ages so green, virgin, young.

And how the ceaseless stream retains

The changeless course, a melody sung.

As changeless, joyous and as pure

I will abide through all future.

I-hwang

청산(靑山)은 어찌하여 만고(萬古)에 푸르르며

유수(流水)는 어찌하여 주야에 긏지 아니는고

우리도 그치지 마라 만고상청(萬古常靑)하리라.

이황(李滉)

20

The ancients saw me not, nor do
I them. Though they are out of sight,
The path they walked still runs aglow
In front o' me. Since the path of light
The ancients fared on lies before,
Why should I waver any more?

I-hwang

고인(古人)도 날 못 보고 나도 고인 못 뵈
고인을 못 뵈어도 녀던 길 앞에 있네
녀던 길 앞에 있거든 아니 녀고 어쩔꼬.

이황(李滉)

21

Hills are spontaneous and free,

So are the sapphire streams that sing.

And shall I an exception be

Beside so many a free thing?

My life was free, so was its race;

My age shall go its own sweet pace.

Gim-in-hoo

청산(靑山)도 절로절로 녹수(綠水)도 절로절로

산절로 수절로 산수간에 나도 절로

그중에 절로 자란 몸이 늙기도 절로 하리라.

김인후(金麟厚)[1]

---

1 앞의 책에는 송시열(宋時烈 ; 1607~1689) 작으로 되어 있음.

22

Mt. Tai-san is a lofty one
But still it is beneath the sky,
However high. If one climb on
And on, he'll top it certainly.
Who must their idleness confess
Prefer to blame its loftiness.

Yang-sa-eun

태산(泰山)이 높다 하되 하늘 아래 뫼이로다
오르고 또 오르면 못 오를 리 없건마는
사람이 제 아니 오르고 뫼를 높다 하더라.

양사언(楊士彦)

23

Have hills words? Do streams airs put on?

Who'll set a price on winds and sell?

Who'll claim the bright moon as his own?

Ne'er caring right from wrong to tell,

This frame that has no illness known

Shall age, in their kind company thrown.

Sung-hon

말 없는 청산(靑山)이요 태(態) 없는 유수(流水)로다

값 없는 청풍(淸風)이요 임자 없는 명월(明月)이로다

이중에 병 없는 이 몸이 분별(分別) 없이 늙으리라.

성혼(成渾)

24

You were a crane that sailed above

The fleecy clouds. What can it be

That brought you down and made you love

To roam this place so worldly to see?

Your feathers long are shed and gone,

Yet lingering here is not done.

Jung-chul

청천(靑天) 구름 밖에 높이 뜬 학이러니

인간이 좋더냐 무슴으라 내려온다

장지치 다 떨어지도록 날아갈 줄 모르는다.

정철(鄭澈)

25

Would that my heart into the moon

Could be transformed, exalted hung

In the blue with no cloudy dune

And represent this speechless tongue,

Flooding with light where my lord lies

Unconscious of my grief and sighs.

Jung-chul

내 마음 베어 내어 저 달을 맹글고자

구만리 장천(長天)에 번듯이 걸려 있어

고운 님 계신 곳에 가 비추어나 보리라.

정철(鄭澈)

26

If tears were pearls and wasted not,

I would store them away and build

With them a castle with a moat

To welcome you in when you yield

To my appeal ten years form now;

But with these running drops, O how!

Jung-chul

눈물이 진주라면 흐르지 않게 싸두었다가

십년 후 오신 님을 구슬성에 앉히련만

흔적이 이내 없으니 그를 설워하노라.

정철(鄭澈)[1]

---

1 앞의 책에는 무명씨 작으로 되어 있음.

27

Rain falls soft o'er the lotus pond;
Smoke swathes the weeping-willow trees;
The boatman is gone sight beyond,
Leaving the boat to breezes' sprees;
Only the listless storks at even
To leisurely short flights are given.

Jo-hun

지당(池塘)에 비 뿌리고 양류(楊柳)에 내 끼인제
사공(沙工)은 어디 가고 빈 배만 매였는고
석양에 짝 잃은 갈매기는 오락가락 하더라.

조헌(趙憲)

28

A hook thrown in the emerald waves,

In a small boat I ride. The sun,

Setting, o'er all its gold way paves.

And hark! the shower adds the fun.

The gleaming things on twigs I'll string

And to yon flowery wine-vill bring.

Jo-hun

창랑(滄浪)에 낚시 넣고 조대(釣臺)에 앉았으니

낙조청강(落照淸江)에 빗소리 더욱 좋애

유지(柳枝)에 옥린(玉鱗)을 꿰어 들고 행화촌(杏花村)을 찾으리라.

조헌(趙憲)

29

On moonlight-flooded Han-san Isle,

In the watch-tower alone I sit

Girt with a sword that gleams a mile,

And resolute belches long repeat.

Hark! someone plays the tuneful flute

And shakes my heart at th' very root!

I-soon-sin

한산섬 달 밝은 밤에 수루(戍樓)에 혼자 앉아

큰 칼 옆에 차고 깊은 시름 하는 적에

어디서 일성호가(一聲胡笳)는 나의 애를 끊나니.

이순신(李舜臣)

30

Incomprehensible! Couldn't I see

That that must needs all come to this?

If I had used a softening plea,

She would have calmed down with a kiss.

This sigh for whom I've sent away

Is beyond me, think as I may.

Hwang-jin-i

어져 내 일이야 그릴 줄을 모르던가

있으랴 하더면 가랴마는 제 구태어

보내고 그리는 정은 나도 몰라 하노라.

황진이(黃眞伊)

31

You boisterous torrent, why so haste,

So dashing over rocky bed,

And boast your speed and pride thus taste?

All's over when to th' sea you 've sped

To turn no more. Then why not stay,

Linger by moonlit hills and play?

Hwang-jin-i

청산리(靑山裡) 벽계수(碧溪水)야 수이 감을 자랑 마라

일도창해(一到滄海)하면 다시 오기 어려우니

명월(明月)이 만공산(滿空山)하니 쉬어간들 어떠리.

황진이(黃眞伊)

32

No fine-sprayed weeping-willow tree

Can bind the passing vernal wind;

No doting butterfly and bee

Can an unfading flower find.

Dear as your love is to this heart,

How can I help it, must we part?

I-wun-ig

녹양(綠楊)이 천만산(千萬絲)들 가는 춘풍 잡아매며

탐화봉접(探花蜂蝶)인들 지는 꽃을 어이하리

아무리 사랑이 중한들 가는 님을 어이리.

이원익(李元翼)

33

You cloud that rest as if to take

Breath before clearing the high pass

Of Chul-ryung, for this exile's sake,

O pray, charge these tears in your mass,

Tears of a wronged one, and them shower

Over my lord's ninefold-walled tower.

I-hang-bog

철령(鐵嶺) 높은 봉에 쉬어 넘는 저 구름아

고신원루(孤臣冤淚)를 비 삼아 띄워다가

님 계신 구중심처(九重深處)에 뿌려 볼까 하노라.

이항복(李恒福)

34

The moon's been hanging like a ball

For ages high up in the sky;

Those storms ought to have made it fall

To rise no more, as one might spy.

And yet eternally it shines

For drunkards and their goblet's lines.

I-dug-hyung

달이 두렷하여 벽공(碧空)에 걸렸으니

만고풍상(萬古風霜)에 떨어짐즉 하다마는

지금에 취객(醉客)을 위하여 장조금준(長照金樽)하노매라.

이덕형(李德馨)

35

Wine's path is no right path, I know
Without your telling me so now,
But tell me what you feel when lo!
A hero's skull's turned by a plough.
A lifetime's short and barren too;
What if this pleasure I pursue?

Sin-heum

술 먹고 노는 일을 나도 원 줄 알건마는
신릉군(信陵君) 무덤 위에 밭 가는 줄 못 보신가
백년이 역초초(亦草草)하니 아니 놀고 어찌하리.

신흠(申欽)

36

Over the hilly hamlet small

Snow falls and hides the path from view.

Leave the gate shut, nor stir snow's pall;

Now none will call, fine had so few.

The moon that rides high in the blue

May be my only friend that's true.

Sin-heum

산촌(山村)에 눈이 오니 돌길이 묻혔어라

시비(柴扉)를 열지 마라 날 찾을 이 뉘 있으리

밤중만 일편명월(一片明月)이 긔 벗인가 하노라.

신흠(申欽)

37

O Han-yang, royal town, adieu!

Farewell, O Sam-gag, guardian hills!

To leave my fatherland and you

Is far from what my passion wills.

Ah! these are evil times ; none know

Whether I shall come home or no.

Gim-sang-hun

가노라 삼각산(三角山)아 다시 보자 한강수(漢江水)야
고국산천(故國山川)을 떠나고자 하랴마는
시절이 하 수상(殊常)하니 올동말동하여라.

김상헌(金尙憲)

38

The peace that holds the mountains still

Cuckoo, why do you break it so,

Still with plaints of a far-off ill,

As if for but a recent woe,

And wake in me disquiet and pain

That won't sleep till I go insane?

Jung-choong-sin

공산(空山)이 적막한데 슬피 우는 저 두견(杜鵑)아

촉국흥망(蜀國興亡)이 어제 오늘 아니거든

지금에 피나게 울어 남의 애를 끊나니.

정충신(鄭忠信)

39

From the famed Hyung-san a rare gem

Unto the market crowd I brought.

Its stony look moved none of them ;

Of what's within they could see nought.

Well, let it lie as if 'twere such

Till knowing people come and touch.

Joo-eui-sig

형산(荊山)에 박옥(璞玉)을 얻어 세상 사람 뵈러가니

겉이 돌이거니 속 알 이 뉘 있으리

두어라 알 인들 없으랴 돌인 듯이 있거라.

주의식(朱義植)

40

I wish ten thousand pounds of steel

Beaten and made into a chain

Endless and strong that I may reel

It off to Sun that runs amain

And in the mid-sky hold him down

For aged parents o' hoary crown.

Bag-in-lo

만균(萬鈞)을 늘여 내어 길게길게 노를 꼬아

구만리 장천(長天)에 가는 해를 잡아 매어

북당(北堂)에 학발쌍친(鶴髮雙親)을 더디 늙게 하리라.

박인로(朴仁老)

41

Don't run because you feel you can,

Nor slowness should give rise to pause;

Be steady in your race, my man,

Incurring ne'er time's precious loss,

For a thing given up half done

Is by far worse than not begun.

Gim-chun-taig

잘 가노라 닫지 말며 못 가노라 쉬지 말라

부디 긏지 말고 촌음(寸陰)을 아껴스라

가다가 중지곳 하면 아니 갈만 못하니라.

김천택(金天澤)

42

As, like an arrow, fleet time flies,

My hair turns gray before I know.

I crop each strand that whitish lies

That I may look young even now,

Lest aged parents see me old,

Grow older, and their own not hold.

Gim-jin-tai

세월이 여류(如流)하니 백발이 절로 난다

뽑고 또 뽑아 젊고자 하는 뜻은

북당(北堂)에 재친(在親)하시니 그를 두려하노라.

김진태(金振泰)

43

Why circle round the lucid sky,

O Eagle? What ! For cold dead rats?

For all the wide ken from on high,

Your view's no wider than a cat's ;

The high-aboded phoenix will

Hold you in scorn and shake his bill.

Gim-jin-tai

장공(長空)에 떴는 소리개 눈 살핌은 무슨 일고

썩은 쥐를 보고 반회불거(盤廻不去)하는고여

만일에 봉황(鳳凰)을 만나면 우읍될까 하노라.

김진태(金振泰)

44

Alack-a-day! Love is a lie ;

That you love me is still more so

And they most grossly truth defy

Who say, "In dreams one's Love will show,"

For how can I who never sleep

Have dreams and there your company keep?

Gim-sang-yong

사랑이 거짓말이 님 날 사랑 거짓말이

꿈에 와 뵌단 말이 그 더욱 거짓말이

나같이 잠 아니 오면 어느 꿈에 뵈이리.

김상용(金尙容)

45

With the sweet breezes of the spring,

Snow is a soon-forgotten thing,

And hills around now wear a face

Refreshing as a flowery vase.

But alas! are there vernal winds

To melt the frost that my head binds?

Gim-gwang-oog

동풍(東風)이 건듯 불어 적설(積雪)을 다 녹이니

사면 청산이 예 얼굴 나노매라

귀밑에 해묵은 서리는 녹을 줄을 모른다.

김광욱(金光煜)

46

You egret that stand on the sand

Far stretching by the limpid stream,

Perhaps you too may understand

This heart that nothing great does deem

That is not pure. In this we're one :

The garish worldliness we shun.

Gim-gwang-oog

어화 저 백구(白鷗)야 무슨 수고 하나슨다

갈숲으로 바자니며 고기 엿기 하는고야

나같이 군마음 없이 잠만 들면 어떠리.

김광욱(金光煜)

47

You restless stream that loudly cry

As skirting this embattled fort,

Why through this sleepless night so fly?

What is the end so madly sought?

This heart that to its lord does go

Day and night, do you vie and flow?

Yoon-sun-do

추성(楸城) 진호루(鎭胡樓) 밖에 울어 녜는 저 시내야

무슴하리라 주야에 흐르는다

님 향한 내 뜻을 좇아 그칠 뉘를 모르는다.

윤선도(尹善道)

48

Whate'er fate brings, sorrow or joy,

I'll never call evil or good.

I am no passing passion's toy ;

To do my best is what I should ;

T'be what I ought to I will learn ;

All else should not be my concern.

Yoon-sun-do

슬프나 즐거우나 옳다 하나 외다 하나
내 몸의 하올 일만 닦고 닦을 뿐이언정
그밖의 여남은 일이야 분별할 줄 있으랴.

윤선도(尹善道)

49

Don't heartlessly brush away the hand
That holds your sleeve. Already the sun
Is level with the grassy land.
As you sit when the walk is done
In an inn room and candles snuff,
You'll what you've done repent enough.

I-myung-han

울며 잡는 소매 떨치고 가지 마소
초원(草原) 장정(長程)에 해 다 져 저물었네
객창(客窓)에 잔등(殘燈) 돋우고 새워 보면 알리라.

이명한(李明漢)

50

The sun sets o'er the westerly knolls,

Blurs all into one boundless whole ;

The moon that o'er pear blossoms rolls

Puts me in mind of one dear soul.

Perchance, Cuckoo dear, you too have

One so to cry for, and so rave?

I-myung-han

서산(西山)에 일모(日暮)하니 천지 가이 없네

이화월백(梨花月白)하니 님 생각이 새로워라

두견아 너는 누를 그려 밤새도록 우나니.

이명한(李明漢)

51

Could tread in dreams leave any mark,

The lane outside your window would

Be worn out like a hollowed bark,

Were it of stone hard as it could.

But alas! no tramp would deface

A dream-way and so leave a trace.

I-myung-han

꿈에 다니는 길이 자취곳 날작시면

님의 집 창밖의 석로(石路)라도 닳으리라

꿈길이 자취 없으니 그를 슬허하노라.

이명한(李明漢)

52

Tell me the worlds before this sun :

Sages and heroes, who were they?

The nations' rise and fall were one

Dream scene that in an idle nap lay.

Then fool is he and wayard man

Who would all leisurely pleasure ban!

Jo-chan-han

천지 몇 번째며 영웅은 누고 누고

만고흥망(萬古興亡)이 수우(愁憂)잠의 꿈이거늘

어디서 망령(妄怜)엣 것은 놀지 말라 하느니.

조찬한(趙纘韓)

53

The sound of passing river showers,
What can it have to so laugh at
That you young holey leaves and flowers
Should roll and shake in glee like that?
Well, laugh and laugh and split your sides,
For Spring, too, never long abides.

Hyo-jong

청강(清江)에 비 듣는 소리 긔 무엇이 우읍건대
만산홍록(滿山紅綠)이 휘드르며 웃는고야
두어라 춘풍(春風)이 몇 날이리 우을대로 우어라.

효종(孝宗)

54

When was the beautiful moon born?

Who first invented this sweet drink?

Ryoo-ryung and Tai baig, both are gone,

Who drank till many moons did sink.

Since no wise man is left to ask,

I'll all forget and drain the flask.

Jung-tai-hwa

달은 언제 나며 술은 뉘 삼긴고

유령(劉伶)이 없은 후에 태백(太白)이도 간데없다

아마도 물을 데 없으니 홀로 취코 놀리라.

정태화(鄭太和)[1]

---

1 앞의 책에는 낭원군(朗原君 ; 李侃) 작으로 되어 있음.

55

My youthful charm's forever flown

In vain devotion ; now I am

A wrinkled wretch, though once well-known.

Would my love eye and know me, came

He here? Should luck me lead to this,

Then Death his sharpest sting would miss

Gang-baig-nyun

청춘에 곱던 양자 님으로야 다 늙거다

이제 님이 보면 나인 줄 알으실까

아무나 내 형용 그려내어 님의손대 드리고자.

강백년(姜栢年)

56

Like his own pupil he me prized,

And I thought such love could not change

With passing years. But I'm despised.

What new love does me thus estrange?

O had he loved me less! 'Twould lend

Less bitter to this bitter end.

Song-si-yul

님이 헤오시매 나는 전혀 믿었더니

날 사랑하던 정을 뉘손대 옮기신고

처음에 뮈시던 것이면 이대도록 설우랴.

송시열(宋時烈)

57

Is not the eastern window light?

The soaring lark already trills.

Does the cow boy regard it night

And linger still in dreamland hills?

Ah! when will he the vast field plow

With furrows long, o'er yon hill's brow?

Nam-goo-man

동창(東窓)이 밝았느냐 노고지리 우지진다

소칠 아이는 여태 아니 일었느냐

재 너머 사래 긴 밭을 언제 갈려 하느니.

남구만(南九萬)

58

A fire is blazing in my breast

And burns up all that's in my side.

Sin-love, the healing god, I pressed

In dream to tell what's to be plied.

"It's a fire," he said, "of love and zeal

For the King ; nothing can it heal."

Bag-tai-bo

흉중(胸中)에 불이 나니 오장(五臟)이 다 타 간다

신농씨(神農氏) 꿈에 보아 불 끌 약 물어 보니

충절(忠節)과 강개(慷慨)로 난 불이니 끌 약 없다 하더라.

박태보(朴泰輔)

59

From napping sweetly by the lyre

Resting from soulful twanging notes

I'm roused up by the barking choir;

It's he who genial mood promotes.

Lad, get the rice boiled soft and fine;

Besides, on credit get some wine.

Gim-chang-ub

거문고 줄 꽂아 놓고 홀연히 잠이 든 제

시문(柴門) 견폐성(犬吠聲)에 반가운 벗 오는고야

아이야 점심도 하려니와 탁주(濁酒) 먼저 내어라.

김창업(金昌業)

60

You egret standing on the ship

That sleeps upon the waves unmanned

Immaculate your body keep.

As pure a spirit, I demand?

If look does not your mind belie,

Your willing pupil here am I.

Gim-yung

빈 배에 섰는 백로 벽파(碧波)에 씻어 흰가

네 몸이 저리 흰들 마음조차 흴소냐

만일에 마음이 몸 같으면 너를 좇아 놀리라.

김영(金煐)

61

I ask you why you linger on

And bloom, O sweet Chrysanthemum!

Summer and spring are spent and gone,

And flowers and dead and frost has come;

Alone you stand to brave the cold,

In pure unchanging faith of old.

I-jung-bo

국화야 너는 어이 삼월동풍(三月東風) 다 보내고

낙목한천(落木寒天)에 네 홀로 피었는다

아마도 오상고절(傲霜孤節)은 너뿐인가 하노라.

이정보(李鼎輔)

62

What I call black they white declare

And white, black. Whether black or white,

The world won't call my judgment fair;

That much is clear. I'll rather sight

Forbear, audition halt, disuse;

This will at least spare me abuse.

Gim-soo-jang

검으면 희다 하고 희면 검다 하네

검거나 희거나 옳다 할 이 전혀 없다

차라리 귀 막고 눈 감아 듣도 보도 말리라.

김수장(金壽長)

63

I'm now old, sick and penniless;

Where are all those that came and went

When I much riches did possess,

And pleasing words so glibly lent?

This stick three feet love is, you see,

All that I have for company

Gim-oo-hyoo

늙고 병든 중에 가빈(家貧)하니 벗이 없다

호화로이 다닐 제는 올 이 갈 이 하도할샤

이제는 삼척청려장(三尺靑藜杖)이 지기(知己)론가 하노라.

김우규(金友奎)

64

O wild goose passing with a cry

In this still, frosty, moonlit night,

As from the north you southward fly,

Han-yang, my home town, my delight,

You must have passed. Then O why choose

To wing on, dropping no home news?

Sung-jong-wun

상천(霜天) 명월야(明月夜)에 울어예는 저 기럭아

북지(北地)로 향남(向南)할 제 한양을 지나건마는

어떻다 고향소식을 전치 않고 네느니.

송종원(宋宗元)

65

I look in what I often did:

Lo! Youth is gone, Age come instead

(Gone faster than the fastest steed!)

Can Youth of his own will have fled?

No, no, you sly old thing! Who else

Has turned him out and brought these ills?

I-jung-sin

청춘에 보던 거울 백발에 고쳐 보니

청춘은 간데없고 백발만 뵈는구나

백발아 청춘이 제 갔으랴 네 쫓은가 하노라.

이정신(李廷藎)

66

If wronged by others, certainly

I shouldn't in evil vie with them:

Forbearance would a virtue be

While vying put me in their team.

Is wrong not on the wronging side?

Why should I mar my case, wrong vied?

I-jumg-sin

남이 해(害)할지라도 나는 아니 겨루리라

참으면 덕(德)이요 겨루면 같으리니

굽음이 제게 있거니 겨룰 줄이 있으랴.

이정신(李廷藎)

67

Dream for me far-away love brought
As good as dead to wakeful hope.
I, passion-mad, like one distraught,
Awoke and scanned all in my scope.
Lo! she was gone, fair child of May,
As if, she, pigued, had fled away.

I-jung-sin

꿈이 날 위하여 먼데 님 데려와늘
탐탐히 반기 여겨 잠 깨어 일어 보니
그 님이 성내어 간지 기도 망도 없어라.

이정신(李廷藎)

68

Spring lingers on bloom-spangled rocks;

The sunset brightens the pine-clad slope;

The meadow is now free of smokes

And adds yon picturesque hills to th' scope

At th' rill-side bow'r I'll lie aslant

Till the moon rise, and poems chant.

Sin-heui-moon

암화(巖花)에 춘만(春晚)한데 송애(松崖)에 석양이라

평무(平蕪)에 내 걷으니 원산(遠山)이 여화(女畵)로다

소쇄(瀟洒)한 수변정자(水邊亭子)에 대월음풍(待月吟風)하리라.

신희문(申喜文)

69

Life is, at most, a hundred years;

Wealth and fame, aren't they but a cloud!

Leaving the world, its joys and fears,

A cot far from the busy crowd

I made my home; hills seemed to say,

"O why did you so long delay?"

Sin- heui-moon

인생천지(人生天地) 백년간에 부귀공명 여부운(如浮雲)을
세사(世事)를 후리치고 산당(山堂)으로 돌아오니
청산이 나더러 이르기를 더디 왔다 하더라.

신희문(申喜文)

70

A dream-seen love is faithless, so

They say. But when I pine and scream

For you who are not near me, O

Where can I see you but in dream?

So, Love, do not call dreams too vain

And show yourself there oft again.

Myung-og

꿈에 뵈는 님이 신의(信義) 없다 하건마는

탐탐이 그리울 제 꿈 아니면 어이 보리

저 님아 꿈이라 말고 자로자로 뵈시소.

명옥(明玉)

71

O let my dreams about you turn

Into a cricket's wailing soul,

On autumn nights when candles burn,

Cry in your chamber like an owl

Till you are rounsed up by the fuss

Who could ignore me and sleep thus.

Bag-hyo-gwan

님 그린 상사몽(相思夢)이 실솔(蟋蟀)의 넋이 되어

추야장(秋夜長) 깊은 밤에 님의 방에 들었다가

날 잊고 깊이 든 잠을 깨워 볼까 하노라.

박효관(朴孝寬)

72

They call me old? Then how is this

That my heart dances still with joy

When a fair flower before me is

And wine is still my spirits' buoy?

My gray hair that plays in the wind?

Well, will it better, if I mind?

I-joong-jib

뉘라서 날 늙다 하는고 늙은이도 이러한가

꽃 보면 반갑고 잔 잡으면 우음 난다

춘풍에 흩나는 백발이야 낸들 어이하리오.

이중집(李仲集)

73

I never thought, you slender branch,

True to your promise, could put forth

So much vitality and launch

Such lovely buds in this chill north.

In candle light I fondle you;

What, my dears! you give odour too.

An-min-yung

어리고 성긴 매화(梅花) 너를 믿지 않았더니

눈 기약(期約) 능히 지켜 두세 송이 피었구나

촉(燭) 잡고 가까이 사랑할 제 암향(暗香)조차 부동(浮動)터라.

안민영(安玫英)

74

The sun sets and she seems to rise,

The moon, to keep a tryst with you,

Imprisoned tree, for with sweet sighs

Of fragrance sealed up hitherto

You greet her; sure, there is a tie,

A secret tie that does not die.

　　　　　　　An-min-yung

해 지고 돋는 달이 너와 기약 두었던가

합리(閤裏)에 자던 꽃이 향기 놓아 맡는고야

내 어찌 매월(梅月)이 벗 되는 줄 몰랐던가 하노라.

　　　　안민영(安玟英)

75

White snow the sleeping earth enshrouds

And hills are alabaster crowds.

Potted plums now are half in bloom;

Bamboos as in a summer coombe.

Lad, fill the glass till — it is full;

For on me is now Spring's sweet rule.

Anon

백설이 만건곤(滿乾坤)하니 천산(千山)이 옥이로다

매화는 반개(半開)하고 죽엽(竹葉)이 푸르렀다

아이야 잔 가득 부어라 춘흥(春興)겨워 하노라.

무명씨(無名氏)

76

Disdain not butterflies, O Flower,

Proud of the beauty that thou hast!

Swiftly will go fore'er thy hour,

Thy prided charm all shorn and cast.

When all thy branches with fruit groan,

They'll come no more, and leave thee lone.

Anon

꽃아 색(色)을 믿고 오는 나비 금치 마라

춘광(春光)이 덧없는 줄 넨들 아니 짐작하랴

녹엽(綠葉)이 성음자만지(成陰子滿枝)하면 어느 나비 돌아오리.

무명씨(無名氏)[1]

---

1 앞의 책에는 이항복(李恒福 ; 1556~1618) 작으로 되어 있음.

77

Suppose spring willows were of green

Gauze made; March blooms of scarlet silk,

Only the great folk's Spring had been,

No flowers red or white as milk

Left to engender clown's gay mood;

Yea, fair is Heaven's way and good!

Anon

녹라(綠蘿)로 전작삼춘류(剪作三春柳)하고 홍금(紅錦)을 재성이월화(栽成二月花)라

약사공후(若使公侯)로 쟁차색(爭此色)인댄 춘광(春光)이 부도야인가(不到野人家)로다

아마도 지극공도(至極公道)는 하늘인가 하노라.

무명씨(無名氏)

78

If weeping-willow sprays thread be,

Bush-warblers fitly spindles are.

And they throughout these spring months three

Have woven my gauze of sorrow. Bah!

My tears are here in leafy shade

As in the flowery season made!

Anon

버들은 실이 되고 꾀꼬리는 북이 되어

구십춘광(九十春光)에 짜내나니 나의 시름

누구셔 녹음방초(綠陰芳草)를 승화시(勝花時)라 하던고.

무명씨(無名氏)

79

O'ernight the wind has scattered peach

Blossoms that shone bright gardenful.

But, my lad; let no broom them reach;

Stir them not with your sweeping tool,

For are they not sweet flowers still,

Although the rough wind blew them ill?

Anon

간밤에 불던 바람 만정도화(滿庭桃花) 다 지거다

아이는 비를 들고 쓸으려 하는고야

낙환(落花)들 꽃이 아니랴 쓸어 무삼하리오.

무명씨(無名氏)[1]

---

1 앞의 책에는 선우협(鮮于浹 ; 1588～1653) 작으로 되어 있음.

🎵 80

Are you a peony or rose

That tantalize my raptured sight

With witching tints o'er you enclose?

I know, he holds you fast by right,

But is it he that owns your charm

Or rather I who feel your balm?

                      Anon

담안에 섰는 꽃이 모란인가 해당환가

횟득발듯 피어 있어 남의 눈을 놀래인다

두어라 임자 있으랴 내 꽃 보듯하리라.

                  무명씨(無名氏)[1]

---

1 앞의 책에는 신헌조(申獻朝 ; 1752~1807) 작으로 되어 있음.

81

I envy much your lot, dear Gull,

Of long, long leisure all to rove.

Your pleasant lore O let me cull,

Where worthy views lie, marsh or cove;

Tell me all and I'll prove a friend

To keep you company to the end.

Anon

백구(白鷗)야 부럽구나 네야 무슨 일 있으리

강호(江湖)에 떠 다니니 어디어디 경(景) 좋더니

나더러 자세히 일러든 너와 함께 놀리라.

무명씨(無名氏)

82

Let us go, butterflies, to yon

Blue hill; you sallow modest one

And you gay spotty, all come on!

When it is late, the trip undone,

We'll pass the night within a flower.

Unwelcome? Then a leafy bower.

Anon

나비야 청산 가자 범나비 너도 가자

가다가 저물거든 꽃에 들어 자고 가자

꽃에서 푸대접하거든 잎에서나 자고 가자.

무명씨(無名氏)

83

Let us be changed in after life,

You become I and then I you,

You pine for me in wasting strife

As I have done all my life through,

And maybe you'll experience

What pain I've borne-my sole defence!

Anon

우리 둘이 후생(後生)하여 네 나 되고 내 너 되어

내 너 그려 궂던 애를 너도 날 그려 궂어 보렴

평생에 내 설워하던 줄을 돌려 볼까 하노라.

무명씨(無名氏)

84

Alas! whom have I given my youth

And whose age have I got instead?

O had I known the ways forsooth

These things so slyly toeing sped!

The pity isn't my darkness, though,

But that to see is vain to know,

Anon

내 청춘 누를 주고 뉘 백발 가져온고

오고 가는 길 아돗던들 막을 것을

알고도 못 막을 길이니 그를 슬허하노라.[1]

무명씨(無名氏)[2]

---

[1] 신명균 편·이병기 교열, 「시조집」 (삼문사출판부, 1948), 218쪽. 심재완의 앞의 책에는, '청춘은 언제 가고 백발은 언제 온고/ 오고 가는 길을 아돗던들 막을랐다/ 알고도 못 막을 길이니 그를 슬허하노라.'로 되어 있음.

[2] 심재완 편, 「정본 시조대전」에는 계섬(桂蟾) 작으로 되어 있음.

85

The lofty pass of Jang-sung-ryung

Even swift winds and clouds need rest

To clear; the spirited hawk that hung

Back at no risk, before its crest,

Stops to breathe. But, be love o'er it

I'll run and slacken not a bit.

Anon

바람도 쉬어 넘는 고개 구름이라도 쉬어 넘는 고개

산(山)진이 수(水)진이 해동청(海東靑) 보라매라도 다 쉬어 넘는 고봉(高峰) 장성령(長城嶺) 고개

그 너머 님이 왔다 하면 나는 아니 한 번도 쉬어 넘어 가리라.

무명씨(無名氏)

86

With my love on my aching back,

Into a burden wrapped and bound,

I stumble along o'er steeps. Alack!

Unknowing friends my groans astound,

Who tell me to throw it away.

If under it I die, nay, nay!

Anon

사랑을 찬찬 얽동여 뒤설머지고

태산준령을 허위허위 넘어갈 제 그 모른 벗님네는 그만하여 버리고 가라 하건마는

가다가 자즐려 죽을망정 나는 아니 버리고 갈까 하노라.

무명씨(無名氏)

87

Shall I buy up love? No one sells.

Sell separation? No one buys.

To induce folk on reason tells

To buy and sell such things, nor lies.

Since this is thus, it is my lot

To love fore'er, yet see love not!

Anon

사랑을 사자 하니 사랑 팔 이 뉘 있으며

이별을 팔자 하니 이별 살 이 뉘 있으리

사랑 이별을 팔고 살 이 없으니 장 사랑 장이별(長離別)인가 하노라.

무명씨(無名氏)

88

Make with a conqueror's sword a bridge,

Over the high-tide-widened sea,

Bent like a rainbow and its edge

So sharp turned skyward, and tell me,

My love is on the other side;

Barefoot I'll crosse it, fear denied.

Anon

고래 물 혀 채민 바다 송태조(宋太祖) 금릉(金陵) 치러 돌아들 제
조빈(曹彬)의 드는 칼로 무지개 휘운듯이 에후로혀 다리를 놓고
그 건너 님 왔다 하면 나는 상금상금 건너리라.

무명씨(無名氏)

89

A needle drops into the sea;

A dozen sailors hotly claim

That each has fished it up with, yea,

The pushing rod. Love, to my blame,

You may hear hundred charges made

But don't believe all that is said.

Anon

대천(大川)바다 한가운데 중침세침(中針細針) 빠지거다

여남은 사공(沙工)놈이 길넘은 사앗대를 끝까지 둘러메어 일시에
소리치고 귀 꿰어 내단 말이 있소이다

님아 님아 온 놈이 온 말을 하여도 님이 짐작하소서.

무명씨(無名氏)

90

The sunset brings me endless sighs;

Cuckoo cries strangely stir my heart.

O rain that fall soft from the skies,

Why should you help the teasing part?

No peace! 'Tis vain to try to rest

When thought of Love must rack the breast.

Anon

일모황혼(日暮黃昏) 되어 천지 아득 적막이라

괴롭다 저 두견(杜鵑)아 불여귀(不如歸)라 울지 마라

아무리 피나게 운들 쓸 데 무삼하리오.

무명씨(無名氏)

91

"What was love like? Round like a ball
Or square? Elongated or short?
Could your arms stretched cover it all?
Or was there much left to be thought
Of?"—"maybe not so long, but I
Cannot tell where its end did lie."

Anon

사랑이 어떻더니 둥글더냐 모나더냐
길더냐 짜르더냐 밟고남아 자힐러냐
하 그리 긴 줄은 모르되 끝 간 데를 몰라라.

무명씨(無名氏)

92

With snow and moon the court is filled;

O Wind, do cease to sough and blow!

No phantasy wild-fancy-wheeled

Could take it for his steps, I know,

But by desire, by burning thought,

Each chance sound into them is wrought,

Anon

설월(雪月)이 만창(滿窓)한데 바람아 불지 마라

예리성(曳履聲) 아닌 줄을 판연히 알건마는

그립고 아쉬운 적이면 행여 귄가 하노라.

무명씨(無名氏)

93

When a flower's seen, you should not cull;

Once culled, you shouldn't it throw away.

To see, to give the clinching pull,

Yet keep it not, is that the way

Of gentlemen? But ain't I sour,

A wayside willow, wall-top flower!

Anon

보거든 꺾지 말고 꺾었으면 버리지 마소

보고 꺾고 꺾고 버림이 군자의 행실일까

두어라 노류장화(路柳墻花)니 누를 원망(怨望)하리오.

무명씨(無名氏)

94

Let benign winter sunshine warm

My Dearest; let the parsley fat

Of spring growth be within his arm!

I know all is his, this and that;

It is my heart, that panting doe,

That can't but be solicitous so.

Anon

겨울날 따스한 볕을 님 계신 데 비추고자

봄 미나리 살진 맛을 님에게 드리고자

님이야 무엇이 없으리마는 내 못 잊어 하노라.

무명씨(無名氏)

95

Butterflies dance before fair flowers

And they smile back their jocund mood;

Year in, year out, their blissful hours

Are thus repeated as they should.

Alas! our love alone, once gone,

Returns no more and leaves us lone!

Anon

꽃 보고 춤추는 나비와 나비 보고 당싯 웃는 꽃과

저 둘의 사랑은 절절이 오건마는

어떻다 우리의 사랑은 가고 아니 오느니.

무명씨(無名氏)

96

Spring showers swelled the streams and lakes,

So you Love failed to come to me.

Summer clouds looked like perilous peaks;

That's how you could not here then be.

The autumn moon's bright in the sky;

Say what you may now, it's a lie!

Anon

춘수만사택(春水滿四澤)하니 물이 많아 못 오더냐

하운다기봉(夏雲多奇峯)하니 산이 높아 못 오던가

추월(秋月)이 양명휘(揚明輝)거든 무슨 탓을 하리오.

무명씨(無名氏)

97

I'll shut my mouth close, shunning talk,

Though sweet is th' lure of tattling,

For if I chat, how can I balk

Harm done me through their prattling?

Since word word breeds and yet none gain,

Firmly I will my tongue restrain.

Anon

듣는 말 보는 일을 사리에 비겨 보아

옳으면 할지라도 그르면 말을 것이

평생에 말씀을 가려내면 무슨 시비(是非) 있으리.

무명씨(無名氏)

98

Let those on pinnacles refrain

From scoffing us that walk the ground.

Theirs is to come down, once they gain

So giddy heights, as years spin round;

Greater aren't we whom future time

May witness higher rise and climb?

Anon

꼭대기 오르다 하고 낮은 데를 웃지 마라

네 앞에 있는 것은 내려가는 일뿐이니

평지에 오를 일 있는 우리 아니 더 크랴.

무명씨(無名氏)

99

Taking a springy, gnarled bamboo

Well trimmed into a fishing rod,

Where blue waves lisp and sea-winds sough

I'll go, fame thrown off like a sod.

Be quiet, Sea-gull; raise no cry

Lest the world should know where I fly.

Anon

소상강(瀟湘江) 긴 대 베어 낚시 매어 둘러메고

불고공명(不顧功名)하고 벽파(碧波)로 돌아드니

백구(白鷗)야 날 본 체 마라 세상 알까 하노라.

무명씨(無名氏)

100

Who can make life of double length?

Several frames have I to spare?

Borrowed is all, health, wealth, wealth and strength

This flesh and blood a dream affair.

If you're so lost on how to live,

When will you life's joys take and give?

Anon

인생이 둘가 셋가 이 몸이 네 다섯가

빌려온 인생이 꿈에 못 가지고서

평생에 살을 일만 하고 언제 놀려 하느니.

무명씨(無名氏)

101

O Egret, do not scorn the crow

For being black. Will dark skin mean

As dark a mind, as fulsome? No!

Cleanly without, impure within

Nothing but you is found to be;

Nay, such you are, or else hang me!

Anon

가마귀 검다 하고 백로(白鷺)야 웃지 마라

겉이 검은들 속조차 검을소냐

겉 희고 속 검을손 너뿐인가 하노라.

무명씨(無名氏)[1]

---

1 앞의 책에는 이직(李稷 ; 1362~1431) 작으로 되어 있음.

102

What ten years' planned toil brought me is

This thatched cot of one single room.

But half is taken by the breeze

And the rest by the moon in bloom.

O where shall I the hills invite?

There let them screen-like cheer my sight.

Anon

십년을 경영하여 초려(草廬) 삼간 지어내니

나 한간 달 한간에 청풍(淸風) 한간 맡겨두고

강산(江山)은 들일 데 없으니 둘러 두고 보리라.

무명씨(無名氏)[1]

---

1 앞의 책에는 〈병와가곡집〉을 따라 김장생(金長生 ; 1548~1631) 작으로 되어 있으나 송순의 문집인 〈면앙집〉에 '면앙정잡가'라는 제목으로 한역가로 수록되어 있어 면앙정 (俛仰亭) 송순(宋純 ; 1493~1583)이 지은 작품임을 알 수 있다.

PART 2
THE AUTHOR'S OWN POEMS
_변영태 자작 영시

우형숙 번역

DEDICATION

Angelic pair, 'tis almost winters seven

Since you so suddenly appeared to light

My groping way to English verse, my sight

So helped as by a shining light from Heaven.

Your words were words of gold ; your silence even

Advised far more than talks oft vainly bright.

These lines may see no light, yet I thought might

Prove a joy 'tween the giver and the given.

May you delight in your tutorial fruit

And more to mend where mending is required,

Purging it from the taint of baneful root,

But, if you by repeated faults be tired,

Be patient as the saints of old who mute

Asked no quick reckoning, deep-faith-inspired.

헌시(獻詩)

제겐 천사이신 두 분, 어언 7년이 흘렀습니다.
두 분께서 천국의 햇살처럼 저를 도와주신지.
제가 영시(英詩) 공부에 매달려 힘겨워할 때
두 분께선 홀연히 제 발길을 밝혀 주셨지요.

두 분의 말씀은 황금과 같았고
두 분의 침묵은 세상 그 어느 말보다 소중했지요.
이번 제 작품집이 보잘것없지만
주고받는 사람끼리 갖는 기쁨의 선물이길 빕니다.

두 분의 은혜로 탄생된 제 작품에 흡족하시길 비오며
수정할 곳이 있으면 수정해 주시되
독 뿌리 오염 털어내듯 말끔히 고쳐 주소서.
미흡한 곳이 거듭 보여 싫증이 나시걸랑
옛날 옛적 성인처럼 묵묵히 인내해주시어
깊은 신뢰로 느긋이 판단하게 시간을 주소서.

🌀 WRITING

Some calm between tempests;

A pool intervening cataracts

Happy with reflections;

A mooring in a harbour,

A sudden home-coming

After wanderings dreary;

A happy moment

Unmarred by chafes past

Nor with future burdened,

When thought, a dust-free mirror

Seeks its own image;

O Pen and Paper,

Slip, softly slip

Into his hand!

글쓰기란

거친 폭풍우와 폭풍우 사이의 고요함 같은 것,
폭포와 폭포 사이의 작은 못 같아서
비쳐보면 행복한 것,
항구에 내린 닻 같고
쓸쓸한 방랑 후
갑작스런 귀향 같은 것,
과거의 노여움에 힘들어 하지도 않고
미래에 대한 부담도 없는
그런 행복한 순간 같은 것,
생각해보면, 티끌 하나 없는 말끔한 거울이
자신의 이미지를 찾는 그런 것이지.
오, 펜아, 종이야,
살며시, 살그머니
내 손으로 오려무나.

TO THE CANDLE

How soft on thy lone altar dost thou burn,
Thou ancient soul of fire!
What mortal can thy tireless prayer learn,
Sweet as angelic choir?
For what celestial bliss dost thou so yearn,
So tremulous aspire?

How gladly flesh to spirit yields in thee!
Yet flesh's not worn too soon.
The best of us still lack thy harmony
And forfeit half their boon.
Thine all-souled flesh, all-fleshed soul let us see,
And hasten Life's high noon!

No nimbus better fits a saintly head
Than thine thy sacred flame.
A sage's life still leaves its earthly dead;
The earth still holds his frame;
His virtue Heavenward soars, devotion-fed;
His clod falls still untame.

양초에게

고적한 제단 위에서 참으로 부드러이 타는구나.
그대 불의 옛 화신이여!
하느님을 찬송하는 천사들처럼 달콤히
지칠 줄 모르는 그대의 기도, 어떤 이를 위함인가?
바르르 온몸 전율하며 솟아오르는 그대,
어찌 천상(天上)의 기쁨을 그리 열망하는가?

그대 육신이 그대 영혼에 기꺼이 굴하지만
그렇게 일찍 사그라지진 않을 걸세.
그 어떤 잘난 이도 그대의 멋진 조화는 못 따라가리.
받은 은혜 절반 정도는 잊고 살뿐이야.
그대 영혼 있는 육신이여, 육신 있는 영혼이여,
인생의 절정기를 어찌 그리 재촉하는가!

성상(聖像)의 머리에 김도는 후광으론
그대의 신성한 불꽃이 안성맞춤이지.
현자(賢者)의 생명은 이 땅에서 몸이 떠나려 하나
이 땅이 그 몸뚱이를 꽉 붙잡고 있네.
현자의 덕이 하늘로 솟구치네, 성스러움 가득히.
현자의 육체는 한낱 미천한 것이런가.

But, Holy Flame, thou art consumed until

No relic's left to mourn;

Only with sweetest memory us dost fill

Of Life not passion-torn.

I ask thee : Whence thy ceaseless, placid zeal?

Of sinless body born?

아, 성스러운 불꽃이여, 그대는 다 타버려
애도할 유품조차 남기지 않는구나.
오로지 달콤한 기억만을 우리에게 채워주고
수난으로도 찢겨지지 않는 삶을 보여주는구나.
나 그대에게 묻노라, 그대의 끝없는 잔잔한 열정은 어디에 있는가,
죄도 없이 태어난 육신은 어디에 있는가.

LOVELESS LOVE ENDED IN LOVE

My wife is a full ignoramus;

She cannot tell her A from B

Yet none for wit and learning famous

Can beat her in heart and making tea.

Before I knew what gamble it was,

Like cocks, us two so set together

Parental edict. (Gain or loss?)

Though young, I full disliked this tether,

But what was there to save a son

From th' arms of maid, an elder by two,

When dad it willed? (You see the fun!)

I married the girl I did not woo.

Free love's as summun bonum held

By all and this they sing and preach,

But hold till you are told, love kneeled,

What I beheld, I you beseech!

I did not sigh away or drone;

A passionate youth seeking an aim,

Manchurian plains I roamed alone

With Bible, heart and manly frame:

Full seven years I spent in the wild,

사랑 없던 사랑이 참사랑 되었다네

내 아내는 학교 문턱도 못 가본 사람이외다.

낫 놓고 기역자도 모르는 사람이외다.

하지만 재치나 박식함에 대해선

아내를 따라올 자가 없소이다 차(茶)를 끓이는 데에도.

무슨 일인지 영문도 알기도 전에

동료처럼 우리 둘은 부모의 명을 이행했지요.

(이득일까요 손해일까요)

젊어서인지, 이런 속박이 참으로 싫었소,

그러나 아버지가 되고자 마음먹고

두 살 연상의 여인에게서 아들을 얻고자 마음먹고

무슨 일을 했을까요? (우습지요)

난 내가 구애하지도 않은 여자와 결혼했다 이 말입니다.

자유연애가 최고의 선(善)이라 여겨집니다.

이 자유연애에 목매이 사람들은 노래하고 떠듭니다.

그러나 사랑이 전부가 아니다 라고 들을 때까지만 그렇지요.

정녕코 내가 봤던 것을

탄식하지도 않고 청승을 떨자는 것도 아니요.

꿈을 쫓는 혈기찬 젊은이었기에

만주 벌판을 홀로 쏘다녔소이다.

성경과 기개와 사나이 기백만 가지고.

7년을 꼬박 허허벌판에서 보냈지요.

She often passing my mind's eye.
Then, coming duty-reconciled,
I began loving with a sigh.

The large difference do you mark
Between the love-making of mine
And that of Cunningham or Clark?
Theirs is to draw the stiffest line
Around their object treated not
As a part of their universe-
Nay, she is th' all-eclipsing spot;
Their souls she can as often curse,
Utterly blight as insected grass.
Homage o'er-paid mines their life-root;
Their zeal to please (how tame alas!)
Too often throws both off their foot.

But mine through love of All I found;
It's not through her that I found All.
Mine wasn't a peculiar charm, gem, sound,
Imprisoning me in a magic hall;
Our union rests on the broader law

그녀가 더러는 생각이 나더이다.
그러자, 의무감에 사로잡혀
한숨 쉬어가며 그녀를 사랑하기 시작했소.

나의 사랑을 커닝엄이나 클라크의 사랑과
비교하면 큰 차이가 있음을 아시겠소?
그들의 사랑은 터무니없이 선을 긋는 것.
우주의 일부로 취급도 안 되는
그런 것들 주위에 선을 긋는 것.
오히려 내 아내는 모든 걸 숨기는 편이지요.
아내는 커닝엄과 클라크의 정신 상태를 꼬집습니다.
벌레에 먹힌 하찮은 잡풀로 시들어가라 욕하면서.
서로에게 지나친 충성 맹세는 삶의 뿌리를 헤칠 뿐이지요.
서로를 기쁘게 하고자 하는 열정이, 슬프게도,
시로를 넘어지게끔 한답니다.

모든 사랑을 통해서 나는 내 사랑을 알게 되었소.
아내를 통해서 알게 된 게 아니오.
나의 사랑은 독특한 매력이 있는 것도 아니고
귀한 보석 같은 것도 아니어서 나를 마법에 빠지게 하지 않소.
우리의 결합은 더 폭넓은 법칙에 의거한다오.

Of human sufferance, the spring
Of conjugal love saved from the saw
Of Time and Freak, part of the ring
Of Universal Love that lasts.
Methinks all men are husband-able;
All women, wife-able, but each casts
All others but one - how reasonable!

Like two gods with no common way
Of communication 'tween and yet
Under one spiritual sway,
We know each other by a set
Of smiles and gestures, for we lack
The common codes of intellect;
This very poverty calls us back
To the Carpentry of the Architect.
Philosophy, my humour keen,
My English verse and all that sort
Are lost upon my ignorant queen;
I make my heart with hers comport.

관용의 법칙이랄까.
시간이 지나도 변덕을 부리지 않는
한결같은 부부애라고나 할까.
오래토록 지속하는 보편적 사랑의 고리라고나 할까.
생각해보니 모든 남자는 남편이 될 수 있고
모든 여자는 아내가 될 수 있지요. 그러나
딱 한 사람만 배우자로 선택하는 것- 참으로 합당한 처사이지요.

서로가 주고받는 대화에서
공통분모가 없는 두 신(神)들 같지만
한 사람의 정신적 지배하에
우리 두 사람은 서로를 이해하지요
미소와 몸짓을 번갈아 써가며.
지성이란 공통분모가 우리에겐 없으니까요.
이런 부족함으로 우리 두 사람은
조물주의 작업에 임하게 되었지요.
철학이든, 유머이든, 내가 쓴 영시(英詩)이든
그런 것들은 무지한 나의 왕비에겐 의미가 없다오.
난 그저 내 마음을 그녀의 마음과 어우러지게 할 뿐이라오.

THE RIVER-SIDE VILLAGE

The haze-veiled crags that stand in rugged strength
Still the abiding autumn tint imbues,
Whose giant race grim guard the river's length,
Whose lingering snow defies Spring's mild abuse.

The river sapphire-hued, a counterpart
Of cloudless sky, encircles the shaggy foot;
And oft a white-winged sail heightens the art,
That glides as if charmed by some magic lute.

Beyond the crags half seen, half hid, lies spread
A cozy strip of land embosoming such
Hamlet of rural name in books ne'er read,
Protected both from fame and sand-squall's touch.

Could one small cot of this snug place be mine,
 The worldly aimless noise I'd fain resign!

강변 마을

안개 속에 울퉁불퉁 솟구쳐 있는 뾰족 바위들
아직도 가을빛 머금고 있고
큼지막한 바위들은 근엄하게 줄지어 강줄기 호위하는구나.
바위에 소복한 잔설은 미약한 봄기운 밀쳐내네.

사파이어 옥색 강줄기, 맑은 하늘 벗 삼아
수풀 무성한 산기슭 휘감고,
신비로운 류트 악기 소리에 매료된 듯
흰 날개 활짝 편 돛단배 유유히 떠가니 더더욱 멋지구나.

저기 저편 낭떠러지 너머 보일 듯 말듯
아늑한 땅덩이 펼쳐져 있구나.
책에서도 본 적 없는 시골마을 감싸 안은 땅덩이,
세상 이목과 모래 돌풍 같은 거친 인간관계 없는 땅덩이.

저 아늑한 땅에 자그마한 오막살이 집 한 채 있다면
세상사 어이없는 아우성에 귀 막고 살 텐데!

TO SHAKESPEARE

For thee there is no epithet correct;
We label all the great in thought and deed,
But thou, more of a wizard, dost not heed
With weird smile, any name we can select.

Did thorny paths of ours, Dread Intellect,
Even thy nicely balanced feet make bleed?
Dark caves of human hearts where deeds hid breed,
Thou layest bare. But who can thine detect?

Deep? No, thou needst not be, for to such eyes
Nothing is deep.Then penetrating? No!
Superbest Mind! all, rendering secrets, lies:
Genius too broadly human to be so!
For aye thy large voice comes as from the skies;
Thy easy grace and wanton laugh we know.

셰익스피어 문호(文豪)께

그대에게 붙여 줄 딱 맞는 호칭이 없어
명실공히 그대를 최고의 인물로 부른다오.
그러나 귀재란 말이 더 어울리는 그대,
우리가 골라준 이름에 겸연쩍어하며 웃지 마시오.

우리가 걷는 가시밭길, 끔찍한 지성인의 길.
그대의 안정된 행보조차 고난의 길이었지요?
동굴같이 어두운 인간의 속마음, 행동으로도 숨길 수 있는 속마음을
그대는 모두 털어 놓았소. 그러나 그 누가 그대 속마음을 눈치 채리까?

깊이 감춘다고요? 아니, 그대는 그럴 필요 없소. 그런 사람들 눈에는
그 어떤 것도 어렵지 않소, 그럼 간파한다고? 아니오!
제 충고에 유념하시오! 모두가 신비롭고자 그러는 것이니까.
재능이 두루두루 인간을 그렇게 되도록 만드는 것이오!
내 말에 찬성하는 그대의 우렁찬 목소리가 하늘에서 들리는 듯하오.
우리는 안다오. 그대의 느긋한 기품과 장난기 어린 웃음을.

JOY

Pluck that flower not;
Let it stay;
Beauty rudely sought
Keeps not ray.

She will droop her head;
Sad new face;
Pretty ways all fled-
Furtive grace!

Touch not, nor profane!
Such pure thing
How can stand a stain?
Die or wing.

Darkness blinds the eye
Of that man
Who'd this law deny,
Dark as tan.

환희(歡喜)

꽃을 꺾지 마세요.
그대로 두어요.
무례히 손에 넣은 아름다움은
빛을 잃어버립니다.

꽃은 머리를 떨구어
슬픈 얼굴을 할 겁니다.
사람들이 잘 모르는 이 묘책
모두들 이 멋진 방법을 포기하는군요.

만지지 마세요. 모독하지도 마세요.
그토록 순결한 것을.
어찌 불결함을 견딜 수 있겠어요
죽거나 달아나 버릴지 몰라요.

어둠은 남자의 눈을
멀게 한답니다.
하지만 남자는 이 사실을 부인하네요.
깡그리 부인하네요.

Orchard not my own
Beckons me-
Charm to him unknown,
Owner he.

Nowhere for the head,
Joy the most;
Sleep on feather bed,
Know the cost!

내 것이 아닌 과일 나무가
내게 손짓하네요.
주인장도 모르는 매력 있는 과일나무.
주인은 내가 아니라 그가 주인인 것을.

머리 둘 곳 그 어디에도 없더이다.
최상의 환희를 위해선
그저 안락한 곳에서 마음 편히 주무세요.
그 보답은 곧 알 것이외다.

I NOTICED A SLENDER PLANT

I noticed a slender plant

With a few leaves round and soft

On a sand hill's sloping brow.

The wind made it bow and dance

Against its will, I know,

For Whene'er the airy motion

Ceased, the blithe stalk returned

To its rightful bearing slender

But noble, resuming the holy

Communion with the sun.

The wind its crown bowed and threw

Against the pointed end

Of a wiry, prickly grass

That hard by spear-like rose

And did not feel the wind.

I almost wept for the plant,

For, though the freedom to move

I have, denied to it,

The wind that blows unseen

Hurls me about as helpless.

가냘픈 풀 한 포기 보았네

모래언덕 비탈에서

가냘픈 풀 한포기 보았네.

동그랗고 부드러운 이파리 몇 개 달렸더군.

바람이 불자 끄덕끄덕 춤을 추더군,

자기 뜻이 아닌데도 말이야.

바람이 멈출 때면

휘청대며 춤추던 줄기가

위풍당당한 모습으로 돌아오더군.

다시금 햇살에 성스러이 반짝이면서

가냘프지만 고귀한 모습이었어.

바람 땜에 머리가 이리저리 마구 움직여져

질긴 가시투성이 풀

뽀족한 끝에 부딪쳐 버렸지.

그것도 창같이 뽀족한 것에 세차게 말이야.

그래도 바람은 자기 한 짓을 모르더군.

난 그 풀 땜에 울 뻔했네.

왜냐면 자유로이 움직일 수 있는데도 난 그 자유를 부인했거든.

눈에 보이지도 않는 바람이

나를 무력하게 이리저리 내동댕이치는 데도 말이야.

THE BABY'S FACE

You guileless yet guileful thing!

Mine must be blind eyes

If they see not now

That behind your wandering but strong gaze

Looks out an old wrinkled face

Telling of old woe and sorrow,

Of old frettings, cares, struggles and worries

Your artless smile,

Your artless throws of limbs

And scores of other infantine graces,

(What a thin-scaled armour!)

All vanish for the while.

Is that your old face once worn and flung

In some remotest notch of time,

Or one that these your waxen feathers will soon overtake?

The old cunning fighter, though under a fresh feint!

동안(童顔)

너 순진해보이면서 앙큼한 것
분명 눈이 있으되 보지 못하는구나
멍하지만 강한 눈초리로
늙고 주름진 얼굴에 씌어진
옛 고뇌와 슬픔, 그리고
초조함, 번뇌, 몸부림, 고민거리,
눈으로 이걸 보지 못하면 사라지리.
순박한 미소와
가차 없는 손짓, 발짓,
숱한 깜찍한 애교들
(이 모두 얄팍한 미늘 갑옷이더라!)
모두 다 한순간 사라지리.
이게 너의 얼굴이냐,
긴 시간 속에 지치고 내동댕이쳐진 늙은 얼굴,
흰 수염으로 곧 뒤덮일 얼굴?
늙었지만 약삭빠른 투사였지, 시늉만 한 것 같아도.

I THEN STOOD HALF IN DREAM

I then stood half in dream,

Listening, listening to a garrulous stream.

But I stood not alone;

Lo! you too fair, free, whispered in charmful tone;

I seemed to hear your voice,

Your notes of friendship in the tumultuous noise.

Ah! then our talk so grew,

So madly that the vale its sound withdrew.

There was a joy profound,

A loud heart-throb; we twin-souls where so bound!

I shook and felt ashamed;

For this sweet useless dream myself I blamed;

I looked up from the brook

And ran my eyes along the hilly nook

Now painted with bright hues

(Autumn her wealth will nevermore so use!)

Again I saw you, Love!

And we, exulting rambled through the grove.

"Let stern Law take his due!"

I said "Our hearts shall roam in bond e'er new!"

그때 난 반쯤 꿈속에 잠겨 서 있었네

그때 난 반쯤 꿈속에 잠겨 서 있었네,
콸콸대는 시냇물 소리를 들으며.
그러나 난 혼자 서 있었던 게 아니었네.
아! 예쁘고 자유로운 그대가 매력적인 목소리로 속삭였지.
시끄러운 물소리 속에서 그대 목소리
그대의 우정의 노래를 들었던 것 같아.
아! 우리의 대화가 후끈 달아오를 땐
골짜기도 숨 죽였지.
진심 어린 기쁨이 느껴졌어
가슴이 크게 요동치고 우리 두 마음은 하나가 되었지.

나는 부들부들 떨었고 부끄럽기도 했네,
이 쓸데없는 달콤한 꿈 때문에 난 내 자신을 비난했지.
시냇물에서 고개를 들어
언덕 외진 곳을 쭉 훑어보았네.
찬란한 색조로 물들어 있더군.
(그녀는 가진 게 많으니 다시는 가을을 그렇게 말하진 않을 걸세!)
다시금 나는 그대를 보았지. 내 사랑!
의기양양하게 우린 숲속을 거닐었지
"준엄한 법대로 할 테면 하라지,
우리 둘은 하나 되어 노닐 테니." 라고 내가 지껄였지.

You sadly, sadly smiled ;

The ocean rolled between relentless, wild.

내 말에 그대는 슬프디 슬프게 미소 짓더군,
큰 바다가 우리 사이에 흘렀던 거야. 무정히 야속하게도.

CHARITY

Smile a genuine smile,
You'll save many a mile.

Try the feeling hand,
You'll find the Heavenly land.

Tend a true need found,
You'll see the world come round.

Have one kind mite thrown,
It will buy you a crown.

자선행위

위선 없는 진정한 미소 한번만 지어요,
숱하게 많은 미소 지을 필요 없을 터이니.

인정 어린 손길을 주어요,
천국의 땅을 볼 터이니.

진실로 어려운 자를 돌보아요,
세상이 돌고 도는 것임을 볼 터이니.

소액이나마 정성 어린 기부를 하시어요,
그 덕에 큰 영광이 생길 터이니.

THERE ARE MOMENTS

There're moments when my very breathing is a bore,

And my own limbs, the fiercest rebels that siege my soul.

How to dispose recalcitrant hands forms a sore,

A terrible civil war that checks a wholesome role.

And there are also moments when I was so bold;

I gobble up the earth, sun, stars, and do not feel

Indigestion; I eat the flesh of sages old,

Both great and small, yet no qualm's felt ; all heal my ill.

Then lo! I feel one mighty Stomach carrying all ;

Then I can live in fire, and fear no gallant fall.

이런 순간들이 있다오

내겐 숨쉬기도 성가신 순간들이 있다오
팔다리가 지독히도 말 안 들어 내 영혼을 피폐케 하고
내 맘대로 안 되는 두 손을 움직이려니 참으로 고통이라오.
끔찍한 전쟁이지요. 안전한 상황을 확인하는 전쟁이요.

내겐 용맹스런 순간들도 있다오.
지구도, 태양도, 별도 다 삼킨 듯 욕심내도 체하지도 않아요.
나이 든 현인(賢人)을 잡아먹듯 힐난해도
크게든 작게든 양심의 가책도 못 느껴요. 내 병 좀 고쳐주시오.
자, 보시오! 난 엄청난 위를 가지고 있는 것 같소.
불 속에서도 살 수 있고 나락으로 떨어지는 것도 두렵지도 않소.

THE SMILING EVANGELIST

Behold her smile! Here is a witness o'God!

What charm, what power and what holiness!

Will you withstand and prove a silly cod,

Or yield obedience to this prophetess?

Welcome, you owner of that winning smile!

Around our hearths celestial radiance spread.

To Him, the Source of your smile, reconcile

The world and me ; now Love through you is read.

What panting, yearning pleading! How it prays!

Yet she is innocently unaware;

Singing and speaking, myriad schemes she lays,

But what can match her smile, a blessing fair?

Beauteous preacher, kneel behind closed door

And plead more for the sinning world with Him.

He who is ever mindful of the poor

Will bless your smile, an answer ah! so dim.

미소 짓는 전도사

그녀의 미소를 보아요! 오, 하느님, 하느님의 증인이 여기 있나이다.
참으로 매력 있고 힘 있고 성스럽나이다.
주님은 이 여성 전도사를 헛된 일한다며 무시하겠나이까,
아니면 교회의 큰 일꾼으로 쓰이게끔 하시겠나이까?

환영합니다. 매력적인 미소 가진 전도사님,
난로 주변에 천상의 빛이 퍼집니다, 그대 덕에.
그대 미소의 출처는 주님, 그분께
저희를 잘 고하여 주십시오. 그대를 통해 주님의 사랑을 느낍니다.

숨이 가쁘고 마음이 끌려 간구하나이다! 하느님께 진정으로 비옵니다.
하지만 그녀는 이를 모른 채
노래하고 설교하며 숱한 계획을 세우고 있네요.
세상 그 무엇이 은총의 선물인 그녀의 미소에 버금갈까요?

아름다운 전도사여, 골방에서 무릎 꿇고
죄 많은 세상을 위해 주님께 간구해 주소서.
가난한 자에게 특히 마음 써주시는 주님이시니
그대의 미소를 축복할 것이외다. 아! 응답이 없군요.

What though our hardened sense wonders deny!
What though our weary mind let trinity go!
But what excuse, if we this sign defy,
To this plain autograph of God say no!

Daughter of Truth! Hail, blissful messenger!
Do mind to pray to smile and smile to pray
Be more than all the ritual that's no spur.
And bring us into Love's eternal day.

우리 경직된 마음이 주님의 기적을 부인하는군요!
우리 지친 마음이 삼위일체를 밀쳐내는군요!
우리가 이 징후를 무시하면
주님의 명백한 응답 'No'에 무슨 변명을 드려야하나요!

주님의 따님이여! 만세, 축복받은 메신저여!
꼭 기도하며 미소 지으세요, 꼭 미소 지으며 기도하세요.
밋밋한 예배 그 이상이 되게 하시어
저희를 주님의 영겁의 나날로 인도하소서.

SOLITUDE

After the day's feverish fray

That must be willy nilly,

Will-harnessed like a warring bay,

Useful yet seeming silly,

What is like thee, O Solitude!

O heal my soul, have gratitude!

I minister oft to doubtful needs

With brave heart but not gladdened;

I ofterner see the husks than seeds;

My soul is sweet but saddened.

But here I see an orb, not an arc,

With all I love, light in the dark.

O princely sumptuous-feasting hour!

O hour of holy union!

O supreme hour of Self's free snore!

Complete without communion.

The world needs me not, nor I the world

Like a lone star in its ring whirled.

고독이여

하루 한바탕 난리법석이 지나가면
반드시 찾아드는 무력감.
모순되는 사태처럼 의도적으로 이용된 것.
필요하지만 어이없이 보이는 것.
오 고독이여, 그 무엇이 그대와 같을까!
내 영혼을 치료해주오, 감사하는 이 마음을 알아주오!

나는 종종 미심쩍은 일을 하게 되지요,
즐겁진 않아도 용감한 마음으로.
그러나 씨앗 속 알갱이보다는 껍질이 더 자주 보이네요.
내 마음이 참 서글퍼지지요.
그러나 여기 생기다만 게 아닌 완전 동그란 구(球)가 있어요.
내 사랑하는 모든 이들과 어둠 속에서 빛을 보게 되네요.

오 고귀하고 화려한 축제 같은 시간이여!
오 성스러이 하나 되는 시간이여!
오 자신만의 자유를 만끽하는 최상의 시간이여!
영적 교감 없이도 더할 나위 없소이다.
세상은 나를 필요치 않고 나는 세상이 필요치 않소이다.
저 하늘 빙빙 도는 외로운 별처럼.

Should Fate so will that she must send
Among the hosts me girded,
With flame and shout to urge an end,
To fateful actions herded.
O let it be, Spitit of Feud!
But spare me inward solitude!

That day with mighty tasks I'll strain,
Risking the greatest gamble,
Yet, if thy sweet song I retain
As in this easy ramble,
I'll walk throught fire and take no harm!
O Soothing Maid, yield me thy charm!

Ere that day come with deafening noise,
Merciless hurl me, fling me,
Tear me from thought and quiet joys
Only this once O bring me
Lone to a grove with starry vault
Or lisping scented sea of salt!

운명의 여신이 너무나 원해
숱한 자들 가운데서 나를 불같이 옭아매어
결말을 촉구하겠다면
운명적인 숱한 행동을 굳이 하도록 하겠다면,
오 나를 이대로 두오, 불화의 여신이여!
나에게 혼자 있을 고독의 시간을 주시오

그날 나는 엄청난 임무로 노력할 것이오.
이판사판 모험으로 위험을 무릅쓰고
그러나 그대의 달콤한 노랫가락만 있으면
이 한적한 산책로에서처럼,
나는 불길 속을 통과해도 다치지 않을 거요!
오 내 마음 달래주는 그대여, 나에게 그대의 매력을 주오.

고독의 시간이 오기 전엔 귀가 아플 정도로 시끄럽길 바라오.
무자비하게 나를 내던지시오. 나를 내팽개치시오,
나를 괴롭히시오. 슬며시 기뻐하며 말이오.
오 하지만 딱 한번만 나를 데려가 주오,
인적 드문 별빛 나는 숲속으로.
아니면 소금 냄새 물씬 풍기는 바닷가로 데려가 주오.

MAGPIE'S NEW YEAR'S DAY

I never knew the beauty hid
In the phrase "Magpie's New Year's Day"
Till, as a lay's refrain,
Again and still again
I heard my baby poet say
The fair words like a bleating kid.

She heard her mother but once say,
When she was cornered to retreat
From an impossible plan
Though planned as baby can,
(Oh, how the old the young wits beat!)
The magic "Magpie's New Year's Day."

Satisfied with this mythic date
Long ere the debt was satisfied,
"Till Magpie's New Year's Day,
Mamma, my hope must stay,"
With rounded eyes grown bright, she cried
Happy as if she gained a state.

까치 까치 설날은

"까치 까치 설날은"이란 구절에
아름다움이 숨겨져 있음을 나중에야 알았지요.
사람들이 후렴으로
거듭거듭 반복해 부를 때
내 딸아이가 그 멋진 후렴을
종알종알 댈 때야 알았지요.

딸아이는 지 어미가 딱 한 번 말하는 걸 들었지요.
아주 어릴 적 계획된 것이지만
불가능한 계획이라 여겨져
취소할 수밖에 없었던 상황이었을 때였지요.
(그 어린 것의 재치가 어른을 이기더라 이거요!)
그 멋진 "까치 까치 설날은"을 이용해서 말이요.

이 멋진 말을 알게 된 것에 만족해
곧 빚진 마음이 청산되었지요.
"까치 까치 설날까지
분명히 내가 원하는 거 잊으면 안 돼, 엄마"
동그란 두 눈을 반짝이며 내 딸이 외쳤지요.
세상을 얻은 듯 기뻐하면서.

Often she climbed her father's knee
With scores of favours for his ay ;
He shook his smiling head,
For they outran her need,
"When comes the Magie's New Year's Day
O won't you get me all?" said she.

A neighbour went away for good,
Taking their baby, mine's close mate.
"Will she be back and play
Next Magpie's New Year's Day?"
Tear-filled, she half cried at her fate,
But soon returned her peaceful mood.

Whene'er Mamma was turned to bay,
Whene'er she saw her faults to mend,
"Then let it be, I pray,
Next Magpie's New Year's Day!"
Thus hopes and sorrows she retained
For the fair Magpie's New Year's Day.

딸아이는 지 아빠의 무릎 위로 자주 올라옵니다.
엄청난 사랑을 받으면서.
아빠는 미소 지으며 머리를 가로젓지요.
아빠의 사랑이 딸아이에게 넘쳐납니다.
"까치 까치 설날은 언제야?
그날 나한테 다 사주지 않을래요?" 딸아이가 보챕니다.

이웃 사람이 자기자식을 데리고 이사 가버린 적이 있었지요.
딸아이의 제일 친한 짝꿍이었는데 말이죠.
"내년 까치 까치 설날에는
친구가 와서 놀아줄까?"
눈물에 뒤범벅되어 딸아이는 슬퍼 울부짖었지요.
그러나 곧 평화로운 마음을 되찾더군요.

애엄마는 궁지에 몰릴 때마다
고쳐야 할 잘못을 볼 때마다 말했지요.
"냅둬. 제발,
내년 까치 까치 설날까지 말이야."
그래서 애엄마는 늘 희망과 슬픔을 함께 지니고 살았지요.
그 멋진 까치 까치 설날 때문에.

NARA

Nara's the soft, sweet heart of all Japan

Full of spruce, noble trees, and meek-eyed deer

That, Nature's moving emissaries there,

Wandering woo the steel fed soul of man.

In these Muse-haunted woods controlled by Pan

Even the Buddhas, that in fanes appear

To meditate, still matchless beauty bear,

Like maiden graces, charm the loose-clogged clan.

No wonder that in dingy Osaka

Damsels as meek, as beautiful and fair

Are oft glimpsed and a vivid fairy land.

Let commerce thrive in modern Nagoya,

But these woods' part shall not be earthly care,

Holily set off for this Samarcand.

나라(奈良)

일본의 심장부 '나라'는 차분하고 멋진 곳.
여기저기 솟은 귀한 나무들, 눈이 순한 사슴들이
대자연의 밀사로 특명 받아
강철 영혼 인간에게 구애하는 곳이구나.

목신(牧神)이 다스리는 뮤즈의 숲에는
불상(佛像)들이 그윽하게 명상하는 듯
청초로이 차분히 더할 나위 없는 자태로
나막신 신고 온 일가를 매혹하는구나.

나무 빼곡히 들어찬 오사카에는
유순하고 예쁘장한 소녀들이 자주 보이네.
생기 찬 요정의 땅이로구나.
현대식 나고야는 상업이나 번창하라.
이 숲만큼은 세속적인 관심사 되지 말지어다.
성스러이 돋보이는 이 숲만큼은.

BIRDS OF THOUGHT

Birds of thought in beautiful
Plumes, come flocking silently,
Some to mock me into a fool,
Some to stay fore'er with me.

Birds of thought alight and go
On their golden-speckled wings,
Bidding dance to the trilling flow
Of their songs a bird ne'er sings.

Birds of thought alight again,
Seeking in my painting brush
Showing as a perky wren,
Or a singer-souled thrush.

생각하는 새떼

생각하는 새떼가 살포시 날아드네.
아름다운 깃털 반짝이며,
어떤 새들은 나를 바보라 놀리네,
어떤 새들은 오래토록 내 옆에 머무네.

생각하는 새떼가 앉았다 가버리네,
끼룩끼룩 노래 부르며.
그 소리에 맞춰 황금날개 퍼득이네.
새는 절대 혼자선 노래하지 않지.

생각하는 새떼가 또다시 내려앉네.
내 그림붓을 뒤지고 있네.
콧대 높은 굴뚝새 같군.
아니 쉬지 않고 지저귀는 지빠귀새 같아.

Wonder-filled I sit and stare
Till the louder birds of thought
Cawing vanish in the air,
Leave me free from all they wrought.

Then the brush begins to move,
Sets me dancing all the time
To the rarer notes above,
Gentler birds' enthralling chime.

호기심이 차올라 앉아서 지켜봤네.
새떼가 더 큰 소리로 지저귀며
허공으로 사라지네.
멍하니 나를 홀로 남겨둔 채.

그때 내 붓이 움직이기 시작하네,
붓 때문에 난 늘 춤을 추네.
하늘의 희귀한 노랫가락,
멋진 새들의 매력적인 선율에 맞춰.

I ONCE SAW JESUS, THE NAZARENE

I once saw Jesus, the Nazarene,

While I cried to the great, heroic Love

Shedding blood on the cross for Sin.

He was still humble, though in Heaven above;

Silently led me to his Faher and vanished, lo!

>   With cross and all.

I found my agonizing soul

Suddenly left before a Majesty,

A nameless purifying Whole

Of Presence; Time, stars, Sun, Moon, Earth and sea,

Like shrivelled skins all hushed and consumed, lo!

>   Man, I and all.

I can't tell which was I and He.

Only I heard eternal "Yea! Yea! Yea!"

In ecstasy. Who could it be

That thus cried? Ah I did not care that, nay!

To be, to see, to know were one. I cared not, lo!

>   Reason and all.

나사렛 예수를 본 적이 있소이다

나사렛 예수를 본 적이 있소이다.
그분의 사랑을 애타게 간구할 때
십자가에서 죄 사함으로 피를 흘리고 계셨소이다.
저 높이 하늘나라에 계셨지만 그분은 여전히 겸손하여
저를 아버지 하나님께 인도해 주시고 아! 사라지셨소이다.
　　　십자가와 함께 말이요.

고뇌에 일그러진 내 영혼이
불현듯 하나님 앞에 서게 되었나이다.
숱하게 죄 사함을 받는 모든 존재들
즉, 시간, 별, 해, 달, 지구, 바다가
오그라진 살갗처럼 조용해지더니 위축되더이다. 아!
　　　사람들도 나도 그 모두가 말이요.

나는 구별할 수 없었소. 어떤 이가 그분이고 어떤 이가 나 자신인지.
단지 난 황홀경에 푸욱 빠져 들었지요,
"그렇도다! 그렇도다! 그렇도다!" 소리만 연거푸 지르며.
누가 그렇게 소리칠 수 있을까? 아! 상관없소이다.
존재하는 것, 보는 것, 아는 것은 다 하나인 거요. 나한텐 그렇소이다.
　　　사물의 판단능력 그런 거 말이요.

When I came to my earthlly sense,

I saw the face of Jesus once again.

Ne'er was my worship more intense ;

(Lord, give Thou me so sweet a rest as then!)

I could attend alike to grass and nations so

       Small after all.

다시 정신 차리고 제 정신이 들자
또다시 예수님 얼굴이 보였소이다.
그때 난 어느 때보다 열렬히 그분을 경배했소.
(주여, 아까와 같은 달콤한 휴식을 주옵소서)
이제 난 잔디에도 국가에도 똑같이 마음을 줄 수 있소
　　　아무리 사소한 것에도 말이요.

MY BABE TALKS WHAT SEEM LIES

My babe talks what seem lies-
Of seen and unseen skies
Of worlds devoid of sighs.

She lisps of fancied toys,
Of visualized joys
That are without alloys.

Also of monstrous fears,
Of what in dream appears,
Unknown to full-grown years.

She such a spirit is;
The sun is than her kiss
No greater masterpiece.

내 아기가 거짓말 같은 걸 하더이다

내 아기가 거짓말 같은 걸 하더이다.
눈에 보이는 하늘과 눈에 보이지 않는 하늘에 대해
한숨소리 전혀 없는 세상에 대해 말이요.

내 딸애가 기발한 장난감에 대해서도 쫑알대더이다.
마음속에나 그려보는 재미있는 건데
합금 같은 불순물 없는 장난감이라 하더이다.

무시무시한 두려움에 대해서도 조잘거렸소.
꿈에서나 나타나는 것
어른들은 잘 모르는 것 말이요.

내 딸은 대단한 녀석이오.
태양도 내 딸 뽀뽀 보다
더 멋지게 뽀뽀를 해준 적이 없소이다.

MOON FROM THE TRAIN

The crescent moon, like a fragmentary vision,
Over things that never stayed,
Chased me and whispering urged my decision;
Softly but madly said,
"Come away with me! I'll laugh with thee!"

She did not seem to know my bounden condition,
That I could not outlive
That uncanny laugh (ah! won't it mean perdition?)
Soon Dawn the veil did cleave;
"Thou hast passed the test! Now see and rest!"

I'm almost glad, I clung to things of earth then,
Unheeding the whispering moon
That threw the mysterious veil of maddening mirth then,
But the echo returns anon,
"Come away with me! I'll laugh with thee!"

내 뒤를 따라오는 달

한 곳에 가만히 있지 못하는 것들 위로
초승달이 부서진 환영처럼 내 뒤를 쫓으며
낮은 목소리로 내 결정을 채근하더이다
부드러이 그러나 단호히 말하며.
"나랑 가자! 내가 너와 함께 웃어주마."

초승달은 내 직분을 모르는 듯했고
난 도저히 그 기이한 웃음을 벗어날 수 없었소이다.
(아! 그런 게 지옥 같은 건 아닐까?)
곧 새벽이 와서 밤의 장막이 걷어졌소.
"그대는 시험을 통과했노라! 가서 쉬어라."

난 지금 기쁘다오, 사실 그때 난 세속적인 것에 매달려 있었소.
그때 그 희한한 시끌벅적 환희를 물리쳐 주었던
달님 속삭임엔 신경도 안 쓰며.
그러나 지금 메아리 되어 또다시 들려오네요.
"나랑 가자! 내가 너와 함께 웃어주마."

A VIEW ON LOVE

He is the silliest of man

Who asks his friends which girl to choose,

Where what his heart will know and can

Is all authority, or lose

He must his sweetest Heaven-sent

Gift, and forever life's content.

Why does your heart grow warm and drunk

Before you open a note from her?

(Blank joy unknown to a real monk)

'Tis more than diamond with you, sir.

You do not care quite what is said,

Yet next morn finds it in your bed.

When you two sit so near and shy,

You can be happy with no talk.

But once you part and days pass by,

You was so bold and no more balk

Writing long letters with no end

On slight occasions you pretend.

사랑에 대하여

그 남자는 참 우둔한 자요
어떤 여자를 고를지 친구들한테 물어보는 그런 자요.
그의 마음은 알까, 알 수 있을까
그의 권위가 어디에 있는지.
분명 그는 잃어버릴 것이요
하느님의 보내준 그 고귀한 선물을, 평생 만족할 그 선물을.

그녀의 편지를 열어보기도 전에
왜 그대의 마음은 따뜻해지고 도취감에 빠질까요?
(진짜 수도승은 절대 모를 그런 기쁨이겠지요)
이봐요, 그건 그대의 다이아몬드보다 값진 것이요.
그대는 편지 내용에 관심 없는 듯하지만
다음 날 아침 그대 침상에서 편지가 발견되지요.

그대 둘이 서로 가까이 수줍게 앉아 있을 땐
말이 없어도 행복할 수 있지요
그러나 둘이 헤어져 여러 날이 지나면,
서로가 대담해져서 스스럼없이
기나긴 편지를 쓰게 되지요.
별것 아닌 경우에도 큰일인 양 여기며.

You know, he must be partially right,

Who once remarked that Love is blind.

Did you not feel your mind grow bright

When in you hand hers lay confined,

Value the Universe again,

And size it truly only then?

At the thought of your darling one

You're tender to a screeching owl,

Manly in trials that otherwise stun,

Generous to all and to none foul.

With such a goddess 'neath your roof,

You feel, you would be quite vice-proof.

You even own that you do see

Some fairer ones, but all you fling

And say, "No! Thisis cut for me

By God, this lovely gem-like thing!

Without her empty would be life ;

All would be mine, were she my wife!"

그 누가 말했던가요 사랑을 하면 눈이 먼다고.
어쩌면 약간은 맞는 말이지요.
그러나 그녀의 손을 꼭 잡았을 때
마음이 환해지는 걸 못 느꼈나요?
이 세상을 다시금 보게 되고
그 순간에 진실로 세상을 가늠하게 되는 것을.

사랑하는 사람을 생각하노라면
시끄러이 울어대는 올빼미 소리에도 너그러이 되지요.
엄청난 시련에도 견뎌내게 늠름해지지요.
온갖 고약한 것들에도 관대해지지요.
그대 집에 머무는 사랑의 여신 땜에
그대는 악에 물들지도 않는 답니다.

그대는 더 예쁜 사람들이 있음을 인정하지만
모든 이를 뿌리치고 이렇게 말하지요.
"아니오! 이 사람이 내게 천생연분이요.
맹세코 이 사람이 진짜 내겐 보석 같은 존재라오!
그녀가 없다면 내 인생은 텅 빈 것이요.
그녀가 내 아내라면 이 세상 모든 게 내 것이요!"

ON THE THREATENED BRITISH INTERVENTION AFTER THE NANKING INCIDENT

The sleeping giant is roused at last,

Following him the hosts of the East,

His slow, sure gait ; his burly cast ;

"Song of East, welcome to the Feast!"

The earth shakes his stentorion voice ;

Advances thus the champion choice.

His yellow armour, helmet, spear,

Escutcheon, and his noble steed,

All one design united bear ;

His battle-cries, too, fiercely bid

"Liberty!" (What sound is so dear!

Ye men white, brown or black, O hear!)

Knights of the West! Knights of the West!

Think well before ye quantlets throw:

Ere rushing to the fearful test,

Mark ye the giant's brooding brow?

For nobler cause ne'er swords were drawn,

And mighty is a thought well sown.

남경사건(南京事件) 후 영국의 위협적 내정간섭에 대해

잠자던 거인이 드디어 눈을 뜬다.
그 뒤를 이어 동양의 여러 나라도 눈을 뜬다.
거인은 느리지만 확신에 찬 걸음걸이로 힘차게 외친다.
“동양의 아들들아, 잔치에 온 걸 환영한다!”
거인의 우렁찬 목소리에 땅이 울리고
챔피언 뽑기가 진행된다.

거인의 노란 갑옷, 헬멧, 창
방패, 기품 있는 군마(軍馬),
모두가 하나로 뭉친다.
거인은 힘차게 외친다.
“자유를 달라!” (참으로 간절한 소리다!
백인이여, 동양인이여, 흑인이여, 그대들은 들어라!)

서양의 기사들이여! 서양의 기사들이여!
그대들이 창을 던지기 전에 잘 생각하라.
끔찍한 싸움에 돌진하기 전에
생각에 잠긴 거인의 안색을 살펴보았느냐?
이보다 더 고귀한 대의명분을 위해서 칼을 뽑아본 적이 없었다.
잘 계획된 생각은 참으로 강한 법이다.

Knights of the West, what do ye find?
A foe! should Faith by Dread be bound,
And nagging Avarice all leave' hind!
A comrade! marching to the sound
Of drums that urge to yon dim shore
You all, despite the surges' roar.

Spare that rash stroke in this dark hour;
Bravely curb your impatient steeds,
When Manhood reigns in fullest power,
Lest you unman these cowardly deeds;
Or should ye blindness ope profess
A soft blow deal; have woe the less.

Knights of the West, if fight ye must,
Keep all the rules of chivalry
Ancient and noble as they are just ;
See your foe armed as well as ye!
And let him pace his charger round
The lists till breathing space is found.

서양의 기사들이여, 그대들은 무엇을 보는가?
적이다! 신뢰는 깨져 공포로 되어버리고
구차한 탐욕이 뒤에 남으리라!
친구여! 둥둥 북소리에 맞추어
저 너머 흐릿하게 보이는 해안으로 행진하는가,
거센 파도가 사납게 포효하는데도.

이 어두운 시각에 무모한 행동일랑 그만 두게나.
그대의 성마른 말(馬)을 과감히 멈춰주게나.
사나이가 최대의 권력으로 통치할 때
이렇게 비열한 행동을 해야만 한다면
그대들이 무분별했음을 세상에 고백하지 않으려면
살살하게나. 슬픔이 그만큼 덜 할 테니.

서양의 기사들이여, 굳이 꼭 싸워야 한다면
기사도 정신으로 규칙을 지키게나,
옛날 옛적 기사들처럼.
그대들만큼 잘 무장된 그대들의 적을 보게나!
적이 말을 타고 천천히 돌아다니고 있네.
휴식시간이 될 때까지.

Shun wily tricks, unseemly sleights

That turn a glory into shame,

That spoil the honour of the knights,

That victors vanquished shall proclaim!

For secret machinations foul

He sees, our dreadful Judge of Soul.

Regard him not as friendless, lone ;

Measure him by his righteous cause,

And by his God who ne'er is prone

To father a cause to end in loss.

Fierce men, let drop the part of Cain!

Dread foes, staunch friends Chinese remain.

Hail! gallant, yellow-armoured knight!

From this shore of the Yellow Sea,

I greet thy mighty form of fight,

And how fain would I give thee knee!

Thy birthright with due pluck uphold

For sons whose number is untold.

교활한 계략, 흉한 책략일랑 쓰지 말게나.
영광이 오히려 수치가 될 터이니,
기사도의 명예가 실추될 터이니,
승리해봤자 패배자라 선포될 터이니,
우리의 무서운 심판자인 그는
더러운 은밀한 모략을 다 찾아낸다네.

그를 친구도 없는 외로운 이라 생각지 말게.
그의 고결한 대의명분을 보고 그를 판단하게나.
그가 섬기는 하느님을 보고 그를 판단하게나.
그의 하느님은 전투에서 지는 이유를 결코 만들지 않네.
잔인한 자들이여, 카인의 모습일랑 벗어 던지게.
끔찍한 적들이여, 지조 있는 친구 중국인들이 남아 있다네.

만세! 노란 갑옷 입은 씩씩한 기사여!
황해의 해변에 서서
나 그대의 힘찬 전투를 반기네.
참으로 기꺼이 그대에게 푹 쉬게 해주겠네.
인원수가 얼마나 될지 모르지만
그대들의 상속권은 마땅히 유지될 것이네.

Dread not the odds thy foes display,

Nor their vain, boasted might of arms ;

Be fearless in this fateful day!

In noble trust that nothing harms

The man who acts the tool of God ;

Thy foes, not thou, shall feel His rod.

그대의 적이 보여주는 이길 승산 같은 덴 마음 쓰지 말게

그들의 큰소리 땅땅치는 무기 따위도 무서워하지 말고.

운명의 이 날에 두려움일랑 떨쳐내게.

하느님의 도구로 행동하는 인간을

그 어떤 게 해코지하겠는가, 믿게나.

그대가 아닌 그대의 적들이 하느님의 회초리를 맞을 것이니.

O GOD!

O God!

Thy fire is spent ;

Thy tent is rent ;

My back is bent ;

My shattered elements remould ;

Thrill this cold clay with interest bold ;

Fix a new soul of kingly hold!

O God!

Thy work is done;

'Tis all or none-

This smallest son.

Nay, I am spent but Thou ne'er art!

Rather play Thine creative part,

And million other ventures start!

오 하느님!

오 하느님!
하느님의 불이 다 쇠잔되었나이다.
하느님의 처소가 임대되었나이다.
저의 등이 휘었나이다.
엉망진창이 된 제가 개조되었나이다.
저의 이 차가운 육신을 기쁨으로 흥분시켜 주소서.
위엄 있는 새로운 영혼으로 만들어 주소서.

오 하느님!
하느님의 역사가 이루어졌나이다.
그것은 전부인가 무(無)인가-
하느님은 안 그런데
마땅찮은 이 자식 놈은 지쳐버렸나이다.
하느님은 창조를 하시고
수백 가지 모험을 하시는데 말입니다!

O God!

Yet leave me not

A broken pot

No longer sought!

O lash me, lash my duty-sense,

That in the end, through fight intense,

I reach Thy good pure and immense!

오 하느님!
그렇다 해도 저를 떠나지 말아주세요
부서진 항아리는
더 이상 아무도 찾지 않거든요.
오 저를 때려주세요. 제 의무감을 혼내주세요.
이제야 한껏 몸부림쳐서
고결하고 큼직한 하느님의 품에 안기나이다.

DAY-BREAK AT MA-HA-YUN MONASTERY

Then in the dawning dusk I was alone

With a bright burning, burning star

Beside a stream that dreamless flows,

Beside a stream that timeless flows.

I wondered and released a human moan,

But from my mind I can not bar

The twinkle of that questioning eye,

The twinkle of that answering eye.

마하윤 수도원에서의 새벽

새벽녘 동틀 때 나는 홀로 있었네,
밝게 불타오르는 별 하나 쳐다보며.
옆엔 냇물이 꿈꾸지도 않고 흐르더군,
무한히 흐르더군.

난 여기저기 쏘다녔네, 신음소리 내가며.
그러나 내 마음속에서 반짝이며 솟구치는
탐구의 눈초리는 막을 수 없었다네.
해답이 눈초리도 막을 수 없었다네.

DEATH

Behind a screen of earth so thin
    Yet deep as death is deep,
My mother lies with settled mien,
    Within a moss-grown heap.

In life she led me, and in death
    As guide before me goes ;
Now unafraid I'll lie beneath,
    My head touching her toes.

I seemed a plant all green with leaves,
    With blossoms here and there ;
Now I'm a spreading oak that lives
    Alike in earth and air.

How holy is the eternal Love
    That binds to mother son ;
That does death's seeming pangs remove,
    And make it with life one.

죽음

죽음만큼이나 얇되 깊은
　　땅 저편에
내 어머니가 누워계시네
　　단아한 자태로, 이끼더미 안에서.

생전에 나는 인도하시더니 사후에도
　　내 앞에서 나를 이끄시네.
이제 두려움 없이 그 아래에 누울 것이네
　　내 머리가 어머니의 발가락에 닿도록.

난 푸르른 식물인 듯
　　내 주위가 온통 이파리와 꽃들로 무성했네.
이제 난 네 활개 활짝 편 떡갈나무,
　　땅에서도 허공에서도 살아갈 수 있다네.

모자지간을 이어주는 영원한 사랑
　　이 얼마나 성스러운가.
죽음의 고통도 없애주는 사랑
　　삶과 하나 되게 해주는 사랑이로다.

TO THE GOAT LIVING IN A STREET CORNER

How is it, you free-footed goat?
  You have a world in dream,
Turn deaf ear to the noise of man?
  Is it the chattering stream
That used to clean your woolly coat?

Elderly, gentle goat, O say.
  The far-off, ringing cliffs
Where you did freely skip and bleat
  O would they heal your griefs
And all your saintly fears allay?

Your silver bleats are no more known
  Nor your large happy stare,
For no more's all that did you good,
  The bracing mountain air,
The leafy view from crown to crown.

길모퉁이에 사는 염소에게

자유로이 오가는 염소여, 도대체 뭐냐?
　너는 꿈속의 세상이 있어
인간의 소리에 귀를 막는 것이냐?
　너의 풍성한 흰 털을 씻어줬던 게
저 재잘대는 시냇물이지 않은가?

나이 지긋한 젊은 염소여, 오 말해주거라.
　저 먼 메아리치는 절벽에서
너는 자유로이 뛰어다니고 울었지 않았냐.
　사람들이 너의 슬픔을 치료해주고
너의 온갖 공포도 가라앉혀 주었지 않았냐?

사람들은 이제 너의 멋진 울음소리를 모르는구나.
　너의 행복에 겨운 큰 눈매도 모르는구나.
너에게 도움이 되었던 게 이젠 없으니,
　상쾌한 산(山)공기도 없고
이 산 저 산 잎이 우거진 모습도 없구나.

All seasons, changes, rain or shine,
  Cruel words or kindly sighs
Are one to you that dream and dream
  With half-closed, blinking eyes,
And think of th' far-off hilly line.

계절도, 변화도, 날씨도
　　잔인한 말, 애달픈 한숨소리도
너에겐 다 같은 거겠지.
　　눈 반쯤 내리깔고 눈 껌벅이며 꿈만 꾸는 너에겐.
저 머나먼 언덕빼기만 생각하는 너에겐.

THE MOOING DISTANT BELL

The mooing distant bell
    Rippling the morning air
So wooingly does knell,
    'Hear me ring; have no care ;
Hear me ring ; fear no Hell!'

저 멀리서 들리는 종소리

저 멀리서 들리는 종소리
　아침 공기 가르는구나.
애잔한 종소리가 심금을 울리는구나.
　'제 소리를 듣고 근심일랑 마세요.
제 소리를 듣고 지옥 따위 두려워 마세요.'

SERMONS TO THE COMMUNIST

The lily, oak and sweet pea equal are

In air and sunlight, if in tallness not,

In quality unique, in kind though far,

In the same pulse of life that has all shot,

A pound of meat would choke to death a child

While a weight-lifting giant surely starve ;

Such equal dealing's something to be smiled.

(Man can be rich in rags by means to salve.)

If others' joys us thrilled as they them do,

Exult then should we everlastingly.

Through pity, love, equality we'll woo,

And in eternal blessings sharers be.

For one more pea, turn up your neighbour's mess,

Be equal just in death and nothingness.

공산주의자에게 주는 설교

백합, 떡갈나무, 콩은 모두 동등하오.

공기 속에서도 햇살 속에서도.

그러나 다른 게 많소. 키도, 특징도, 생각도,

도전하는 삶의 의향도 똑같진 않소.

고기 한 덩어리에 역도 선수는 허기지지만

어린 꼬마는 그 고기가 목에 걸려 죽을 수도 있소.

똑같은 대우, 똑같은 분배는 어처구니없는 일이요.

(인간은 누더기 걸친 부자일 수 있소. 위로 받으려고 누더기를 걸

친 것이요)

다른 사람의 기쁨이 우리를 진실로 감동시킨다면

우린 영원히 기뻐 날뛰어야 하겠지요.

우리 모두가 갈구하는 동정심, 사랑, 동등함을 통해

우리는 서로 공유하여 영원한 축복을 누려야 하겠지요.

하지만 콩 한쪽 더 가지려고 해보시요. 이웃이 가만있지 않을 거요.

다들 똑같이 동등하게 죽는 거지요. 허망한 거지요.

Freedom divested, can man still be man?

He's given the regal will to choose between

Heaven and Hell, and, argue what you can,

Heaven would not be such, were forced he in.

Man is created to ceate (mark this!)

Will-less creators! Monstrous mockery!

Take the free will from man, and God will cease ;

His whole creation will a void blank be.

Who are you gawky darkling quibbling guys

That hold that man is nothing but state all?

Man must do what is told him to with sighs

And what you-guys-pulled "state" thinks his own call!

After this topsyturvy notion hanker ;

You will be on civilization canker.

자유가 박탈되는 데도, 인간이 여전히 인간이겠소?

인간은 당당히 선택권이 있는 거요.

천국과 지옥을 선택할 권리요.

그대들이 뭐라 주장해도 하늘은 그대들 뜻과 다르오.

인간은 창조되어 태어난 것이요(이 점을 명심하시오!)

의지를 작용시키지 않는 그대들! 조롱거리밖에 안 되는 것이오!

인간에게서 자유의지를 빼앗아 보구려. 그러면 하느님이 역사하시
질 않을 것이요.

하느님의 창조활동은 모두 공백상태가 될 것이요.

인간은 '국가'일 뿐이라 주장해대는

얼빠진 그대, 말 둘러대는 그대, 그대들은 누구인가?

인간은 자기가 들은 것을 한숨 쉬면서도 하는 법이요.

그대들이 끌어다 댄 "국가"를 인간은 소명이라 생각할 수도 있소.

이 뒤죽박죽 이념을 탐낸다면

그대들은 사회의 악이 될 것이요.

Whene'er I pass by shops that line the streets
Or those that, where they can, themselves ensconce,
Whether in lanes that seldom ring with beats
Of shoppers' feet or chats and their response,
Or any unfrequented villages,
All decked with nick-nacks, kept so neat and trim,
Alluring one into lust to possess
The things made to his varying taste or whim,
This query creeps uncalled into my mind:
Will you, Commissars, if you to your own
Come, sweep away all these, and power find,
Attend to us with care and fondness known?
Won't you, monopolizing human trust,
Denying Man and Freedom, bring rust, dust?

거리에 죽 늘어선 가게를 지나칠 때마다,
잘 보이지 않는 가게를 지나칠 때마다,
손님의 발자국 소리, 손님의 주고받는 얘기 소리가
별로 들리지 않는 길에서건
인적 드문 마을에서건
장신구가 깔끔히 잘 즐비 되어 있음을 본다오.
손님을 꾀어 사고 싶게끔
손님 취향 따라 만들어진 물건들이요.
미심쩍은 생각이 드오. 원치 않아도.
그대, 인민 위원들이여, 어서 이리로 와
이 모든 것들을 없애고 힘을 얻어
우리 마음에 들도록 우리를 신중히 돌보아 주겠소?
우리 인간의 신뢰를 독점한 뒤 인간과 자유를 부인하고
하찮은 부패 따윈 가져오진 않을 거지요?

APOLOGIA FOR E. D.

Why, had an angel babbled half as well,

Would you have nudged her to clearer tell?

Heavenly Beings're usually so dumb ;

What! have this talking angel beat the drum!

Her English grammar rouses your concern?

Yes, I admit her scornful twist and turn.

Current too strong its dams may overbound ;

Seraphic thoughts should have tame channels found!

And then the rhyme! You point the damage done?

With all your wails and cares, I say, be gone!

Ever so fresh, e'er new as morning dew

Fore'er her music will daze me and you.

Fresh now and fresh a thousand years from now,

Maybe a million years hence. You ask how?

The change of language, in the normal course,

Will a far longer time require, perforce,

To overtake her; it is how she'll shine

As racy through all time without a sign

Of going stale. But woe to imitators ;

They'll go to Jericho, rot like potatoes.

A gem the mire encasing glorifies ;

A fault without her worth forgotten dies.

E. D. 를 위한 변호

이런, 천사가 어설프게 말했다면

천사가 더 명확히 말하도록 자극해 주셨어야지요?

착한 사람들은 멍청한 면이 있거든요.

뭐라고요! 말하는 천사가 항의를 했다고요!

그녀의 영어 문법이 당신의 감정을 자극한다고요?

예, 저도 인정합니다, 그녀의 천방지축을.

물살이 너무 심해 댐이 넘실댈 지경처럼 걱정스럽죠.

착한 생각이었다면 평탄한 경로를 찾아야 했었는데.

그 다음 운(韻)은요! 당신이 그 피해를 지적하십니까?

당신의 한탄과 걱정은 접어 두시오.

아침이슬처럼 신선하고 새롭게

그녀의 소리는 나와 당신을 영원히 매료시킬 것이요.

지금도 그리고 앞으로 천 년 후까지도 신선하게 말이요.

아마 백 만년 이후에도 그럴 것이요. 어떻게 그러냐고요?

언어가 바뀌어 정상적인 경로로

그녀를 따라잡자면 반드시 숱한 세월이 흘러야 하오.

그래서 그녀는 늘 빛날 것이요

사그라질 기미도 없이. 그러나 모방자들에겐 슬픈 일이요.

모방자들은 감자처럼 썩어빠져 제리코에게 갈 것이요.

보석은 그 주위의 진흙을 영화롭게 하는 법이지요.

그녀의 결점은 잊혀져 사라지겠지요.

TO EMILY DICKINSON

Thy songs are pearls, and what art thou?
    Thy name is Purity!
O virgin singer, let me bow
    In reverence to thee.

Raised planes reduce to crouching knolls
    The lofty-seeming hills,
Mississippis with stately rolls
    To mere meand'ring rills.

A courtier Chaucer is doubtless ;
    Worldly looks Shakspeare e'en ;
What's Browning? Country parson, yes,
    To thine angelic sheen.

에밀리 디킨슨 시인께

그대의 노래는 진주입니다. 그대는 어떤 사람이죠.
　　그대는 일명 '순결함'이지요!
오 순결하게 노래하는 이여, 고개 숙여
　　그대를 경배하나이다.

높이 나는 비행기에서는
　　우뚝 솟은 산도 웅크린 둔덕처럼 작아 보이고
당당히 굽이쳐 흐르는 미시시피 강도
　　꼬불꼬불 실개천으로 작아 보이죠.

그대의 반짝이는 성스러움에 비하면
　　쵸서는 분명 아첨꾼,
셰익스피어는 세속적으로 보이죠.
　　브라우닝은 어떠냐고요? 그냥 시골 목사죠. 네.

Poet Supremest! Sappho's aid,
    High culture, (ah! forsooth)
To thee a hindrance might have made,
    A tomb, not door, to truth.

A stained glass but itself displays,
    Impeding, marring light.
O Crystal Soul! thee nothing pays
    That keeps pure truth from sight.

최상의 시인이시여! 그리스 시인 사포의 도움으로
　　고매한 고양 있는 분 (아! 정말이요)
그대에게 장애물이란 진리로 향하는 문이 아닌
　　진리를 매장하는 것이었을 거요.

스테인드 글라스는 자체 모습만 보여줄 뿐
　　빛을 못 들어오게 방해하지만,
오, 수정같이 해맑은 그대! 그대는 정녕코
　　순수한 진리를 우리 눈앞에 보여주는 분이라오.

TO THE SAME

Holy angel, who art thou?
    Art thou Dickinson?
Art thou God's sweet darling now
    As on earth, O Nun?

Devil smote thy wings of Dove?
    Offered thee his crutch;
Rather chos'st thou not to move,
    So thou shunnedst his clutch.

Life to thee came as a wound,
    Left thee as a scar,
Not a blotch, as it thee found,
    Sweetest sad bright star!

같은 분(에밀리 디킨슨)께

하늘의 천사여, 그대는 누구십니까?
　　그대, 디킨슨이신가요?
그대, 하느님이 지극히 사랑하는 분
　　이 지상에서 수녀님이신가요?

악마가 비둘기였던 그대의 날개를 쳐서
　　그대에게 자기 목발을 주었지요.
그러나 그대는 악마의 목발을 멀리 했어요.
　　차라리 움직이지 않겠다 작정하시고.

그대에게 인생은 상처로 다가왔고
　　그대에게 흉터를 남겼지요.
그 흉터가 그대에겐 흠이 아니라
　　서럽도록 예쁜 밝은 별입니다.

Popes and prelates knew thee not ;
   They were so afraid
Ofthy pious flouts; thy lot,
   Loneliness, thou paid.

Thou art God's sweet darling now
   'Bove our shining sun.
As I thee, wilt thou me know
   When my race is run?

교황님도 성직자들도 그대를 몰랐지요.
　　그분들은 그대의 힐난을 아주 두려워했지요.
그대는 그대의 운명인
　　바로 그 외로움을 표시한 거였지요.

그대는 저 빛나는 태양 위에서
　　하느님이 지극히 아끼시는 분.
나, 그대를 알건만, 그대는 나를 알까요.
　　나의 일이 진행될 때 말이요.

THE CHICK

Once landed shy a chick
On my flat bony hand
By chance put on the floor,
Tho' nothing's there to pick.
The speck of life I scann'd,
Throbbing to its core.

The life-thrilled claws of Chick
Something warm seemed to find;
"Grow and be strong," said I,
"That you may beak and kick,
Lone thing, among your kind,
I will soon set you free."

"The mewing prowling puss,
The wheeling screaming bird,
The humming stinging bee
In vain shall make such fuss ;
I, chick of God, our Herd,
Shall your protector be."

병아리

쫘악 편 내 손 위로
병아리가 수줍은 듯 다가온 적 있다네.
행여 마룻바닥인가 하여 온 게지.
쪼아 먹을 게 없는데도 말이야.
뼛속까지 흥분하며
그 생명체를 찬찬히 훑어보았지.

병아리가 생명감 넘치는 발톱으로
따끈한 뭔가를 찾는 듯 했어.
난 한마디 했지.
"강하게 자라거라, 친구들 틈에서.
외로움일랑 부리로 쪼아내고 발로 차 버려라.
내가 너를 곧 놓아 주마."

"야옹대며 돌아다니는 고양이,
짹짹대며 빙빙 날아다니는 새,
붕붕대며 찔러대는 벌,
이들은 설쳐 봤자 허사다.
내가 너의 보호자 되어 줄 거니까
우리 주, 하느님이 아끼시는 병아리야."

APPENDIX

BIOGRAPHICAL NOTES

on
The author's of the old songs,
arranged in alphabetical order

SONGS FROM KOREA

AN MIN YUNG Nothing is definitely known except that his close friends called him by the name of Hyung-bo. (See poems 73, 74)

안민영(安玟英) : 친구들 사이에서 형보(荊甫)란 이름으로 불렸고 그 외엔 알려진 바 없음.

BAG HYO GWAN Nothing is known of him except that intimate friends used to call him Ja-hwa. (See poem 71)

박효관(朴孝寬) : 친구들 사이에서 자화란 이름으로 불렸고 그 외엔 알려진 바 없음.

BAG IN LO He was an army officer in the reign of King Sun-jo whose rule lasted from 1568 to 1608. (See poem 40)

박인로(朴仁老) : 선조(재위기간 1568-1608) 때의 무관.

BAG TAI BO (1664~1689)   Bag-tai-bo passed the Civil Service Examination at the top. By writing to King Soog-jong to desist from sending away hisqueen, he incurred the royal displeasure and underwent tortures in the presence of the King. He did not lose his head in the midst of the tortures and answered the King's questions as if nothing were happening. He did not survive them many hours, however, losing too much blood. (See poem 58)

박태보(朴泰輔 ; 1664~1689) : 과거시험에서 장원급제를 했음. 숙종이 왕비를 폐했을 때 불가함을 아뢰는 상소를 올렸다가 왕의 진노를 샀으며 왕의 목전에서 고문을 당함. 모진 고문에도 굴하지 않고 왕의 질문에 꼿꼿이 답하였으며 과다 출혈로 인해 고문 받는 중에 사망함.

BYUN GYE RYANG (1369~1430) Toward the close of the Go-ryu Dynasty he obtained a government position through Civil Service Examination. When the I Dynasty discarded the old one, he again sought fortune, passing the qualifying examination again under the new regime. His literary talent was unchallenged. In the matter of letters, the King relied solely on him. In one instance, he upheld his opinion in utter disregard to all his other counsellors' unanimous one. He rose to the high position of Grand Master of Learning, which he held for an unusually long period. (See poem 5)

변계량(卞季良 ; 1369~1430) : 고려 말엽, 과거에 급제하여 관직 얻음. 고려왕조가 없어지고 조선왕조가 섰을 때 다시 좋은 성적으로 과거시험에 합격함. 문장력이 매우 출중하여 왕에게 전적으로 신뢰를 받음. 일례로, 왕이 조정신하들의 만장일치된 의견을 묵살하고 변계량의 의견을 받아들인 바도 있음. 대제학까지 벼슬을 지녔으며 비교적 장기간 그 자리를 향유함.

GANG BAIG NYUN In 1627 Gang-baig-nyun passed the Civil Service Examination at the top. He became the head of the Board of Counsellors. He wrote several books. (See poem 55)

강백년(姜栢年) : 1627년, 과거시험에서 장원급제함. 벼슬이 판중추부사(判中樞府事)에까지 이르렀으며 저서 몇 권을 남김.

GIL JAI (1352~1418) IN 1386 Gil-jai passed the Civil Service Examination under the declining Go-ryu regime and began to climb the ladder of distinction and power, when the King whom he was serving was deposed on the ground of illegitimacy. He retired then and there. When he was only seven years old, he was left to live with his maternal grandmother, his father removed to a distant post which did not bring enough to support all the family. He was one day observed to prattle to the turtle he had caught :

> Dear turtle, turtle dear,
> O have you lost your ma?
> Why stray so far as here?
> I too have lost my ma.
>
> I know what cooks may say,
> But go! I set you free.
> Our mas are far away.
> Go, turtle, and be free!

He let the turtle go and burst out crying. A looker-on ran up, it is said, and hugged him crying too. His later life proved that he had a great affection for his mother. Though he himself refused to serve the I Dynasty, he allowed his son the accept the offer of a government position, saying with feeling, "Son, be as loyal to your King as I have been to my Go-ryu King." When he fell seriously ill just before his end, his wife asked him whether his son should be told. "No," said he, "he is in the King's service. It is enough to let him know when I am gone." (See poem 6)

길재(吉再 ; 1352～1418) : 1386년, 고려 말엽 과거시험에 합격하여 높은 벼슬에 오름. 모시던 왕이 서출(庶出)이라는 이유로 퇴위되자 관직에서 물러남. 7세 때에는 외조모와 기거하게 되었는데 부친이 한직으로 물러나 식솔을 거느리기가 어려웠기 때문임. 하루는 거북이를 잡고 다음과 같이 말했다고 함.

> 거북아, 거북아
> 엄마를 잃었니?
> 왜 이리 멀리 와서 헤매니?
> 나도 엄마가 없단다.
>
> 요리사들이 뭐라 말할지 난 알아.
> 가거라! 너를 놓아주마.
> 우리 엄마들은 머나먼 곳에 있단다
> 가거라. 거북아, 너를 놓아주마.

이 거북이를 놓아준 뒤 목놓아 울었는데 구경꾼이 달려와 안아주었다고 함. 말년에는 어머니에 대한 강한 애정을 보였다고 함. 본인은 조선왕조에 벼슬하기를 거부했지만 아들이 관직에 오르는 것은 허락했다고 함. "아들아, 내가 고려왕께 충성했듯이 너도 너의 왕께 충정을 다하거라."고 일러주었음. 임종하기 전 심히 아플 때 아내가 아들을 부를까 여쭈어 보자 다음과 같이 말했다고 함. "지금 아들은 왕을 보필중이니 내 임종을 말하지 말고, 내가 죽고 나거든 알리시오."

GIM CHANG UB (1658~1721) As a child Gim was regarded as a phenomenon. His understanding of difficult passages in classics was something marvellous. He could write excellent poems, too. But, however, he was too chauvinistic and free-spirited to settle down to the sleek official life. He was indifferent to fame and wealth. He was rather bent upon leading a leisurely, secluded life after the fashion of many illustrious ancients. He declined the offer of an official position of some importance. (See poem 59)

김창업(金昌業 ; 1658~1721) : 소싯적에 이미 천재로 알려짐. 어려운 고전 문구도 남달리 탁월하게 이해를 잘했으며 문장력이 출중한 시를 쓰기도 했음. 그러나 너무 방랑벽이 있어 그럴듯한 공직 생활에 안착 하지 못했음. 명예나 부에 관심이 없었고 몇몇 옛 기인처럼 한적한 은 둔 생활을 영위했음. 중요 관직을 제의받았으나 거절함.

GIM CHUN TAIG He was a police-sergeant during the reign of King Soog-jong, that is, some time between 1675 and 1720.
(See poem 41)

김천택(金天澤) : 숙종(재위기간 1675~1720) 때의 무관.

GIM GWANG OOG (1580~1656) Gim seems to have been a blunt robust man of foresight. His bluntness of speech in the court often nearly cost him neck, but it was simply out of honesty and vigour. He always sided with the upright and public-spirited. He was promoted Royal Counsellor in the end. He wrote many songs.
(See poems 45, 46)

김광욱(金光煜 ; 1580~1656) : 앞을 내다보는 선견지명이 있으며 강인 하고 무뚝뚝했다고 함. 조정에서 언사가 통명하여 목이 날아갈 뻔한 때가 자주 있었다고 함. 그런 통명한 언사는 정직함과 기백에서 비롯 되었다 함. 항상 올곧고 애국심 있는 자들 편에 섰다고 함. 왕의 자문 역할을 할 수 있는 요직을 두루 거쳤으며 많은 작품을 남김.

GIM IN HOO (1510~1560)   As might be expected from one profound in learning, Gim-in-hoo was serene and meditative. He used to sit up whole nights lost in thinking. In 1540 he passed the Civil Service Examination. A rate friendship sprang up between him and the Crown Prince who later became King In-jong. He saw in the prince the making of a great monarch and expected great things of him. But not more than several months after the accession, the much looked-forward-to regin of In-jong was cut short by his sudden death. The sad news sent Gim into a swoon, who was then a Country Governor. He resigned and never accepted any appointment again. He did not survive the blow many years. On every death anniversary of his lord, he betook himself to the mountains to lament there until sunset. He was noted for facial beauty and brightness. His pen name was Ha-su. (See poem 21)

김인후(金麟厚 ; 1510~1560) : 학문이 깊었던 점으로 미루어보아, 작가는 차분하고 묵상형이었다고 보여짐. 사색에 잠겨 밤을 지새기 일쑤였다고 함. 1540년, 과거 급제함. 후일 인종이 되신 세자와 남다른 교분이 있었고 세자에게서 참된 군주의 면모를 보고 큰 기대를 했었음. 그러나 왕위 등극 몇 달도 되지 않아 기대에 어긋나게 인종이 급사함. 이 비보를 듣고 졸도함. 당시의 벼슬은 한 지방 관아의 우두머리였는데 이 관직을 사임하고 이후에 어떤 관직도 받지 않았음. 몇 년 동안 그 충격에서 헤어나지 못함. 인종 기일에는 매번 산에 들어가 해질녘까지 인종을 애도했음. 미남이었고 총명했다고 알려짐. 호는 하서(河西).

GIM JIN TAI He was a contemporary of King Soog-jong whose reign lasted from 1675 to 1720. (See poem 42, 43)

김진태(金振泰) : 숙종(재위기간 1675~1720) 때 사람.

GIM JONG SU In 1405 he passed he Civil Service Examination. He was short of stature, but unusually sagacious. He reclaimed a wide tract out of the no man's land between Korea and China, and established six new border fortress towns. While he was Left Associate Premier, Grand Prince Soo-yang-dai-goon, who later assumed the royal title of Se-jo, killed him out of his way to the throne on the very eve of his accession. (See poem 8)

김종서(金宗瑞) : 1405년, 과거에 급제. 키가 작았으나 빈틈이 없었다고 함. 중국과의 국경 지역에 소유주가 없는 땅을 개간하여 요새 형태의 큰 부락을 만듦(육진 개척). 좌의정으로 있을 때 수양대군(후일 세조가 됨)에게 피살됨. 세조 등극하기 바로 전날 밤의 일이었고 피살 사유는 세조 등극 반대였음.

GIM OO GYOO Nothing is known of him. (See poem 63)

김우규(金友奎) : 작가에 대해 알려진 바가 없음.

GIM SANG HUN (1570~1652) The Civil Service Examination opened a career for Gim-sang-hun as for many others. He successively became Grand Master of Learning, Minister of Ceremonies, Right and Left Associate Premier. When he was Minister of Ceremonies, the Manchus invaded. The King and his court had to shut themselves in Nam-han-san-sung, a mountain fastness. At length, peace was decided upon and the treaty was drawn. It was a sort of surrender. Gim tore up the shameful instrument and burst into lamentation. One of his colleagues dragged him away calling him a patriot. Manchus took him to Mukden and imprisoned him three years. They relented, however, and released him, perhaps from respect for his letters, which were unrivalled in his own times. His poem here given was apparently written just before his departure for Mukden. (See poem 37)

김상헌(金尙憲 ; 1570~1652) : 많은 사람들이 그러했듯이 과거 급제하여 벼슬길에 오름. 대제학, 예조판서, 우의정과 좌의정을 역임. 예조판서로 봉직할 때 만주 방면에서 이민족(청나라)이 쳐들어와(병자호란) 왕이 신하들과 남한산성에 피난가게 됨. 종국에는 평화조약을 체결하게 되나 일종의 치욕적인 조약이었음. 김상헌은 치욕스런 체결문을 찢으며 오열했고 조정관료 중 한 명이 그를 애국자라 일컬으며 밖으로 끌고 나갔다고 함. 침략자들은 그를 묵덴(일명 심양)이란 곳으로 끌고 가 3년간 감옥살이를 시켰음. 그러나 타의 추종을 불허하는 탁월한 문장력에 감화를 받은 침략자들이 그를 방면해 주었다고 함. 이 책에 실린 작품은 묵덴을 향해 출발하기 바로 전에 남긴 것.

GIM SANG YONG (1561~1637) In the year 1632 Gim-sang-yong was made Right Associate Premier. During the Manchu Invasion in 1636, he followed the royal ancestral tablets and the Crown Prince to the island of Gang-hwa to seek safety there. When the island was taken by the enemy, he who had never smoked ordered pipe and match to be brought. He killed himself by setting fire o a bundle of powder. In remembrance of his martyrdom, the king conferred he

Loyalty Gate on his family. (See poem 44)

김상용(金尙容 ; 1561~1637) : 1632년, 우의정에 오름. 1636년, 병자호란 때 묘사주(廟社主)를 받들고 세자를 수행하여 강화도로 피난. 강화도가 침략군에 함락되자 담배를 하지 않았던 그가 담배와 불을 가져오라 이르고 화약에 불을 질러 자결함. 그의 순국을 기리기 위해 왕이 정려문(旌閭門)을 세워줌.

GIM SOO JANG   He was a small official in the time of King Soog-jong, who reigned from 1675 to 1720. His pen name was No-ga, meaning "old song."Numerous songs of his are on record. (See poem 62)

김수장(金壽長) : 숙종(재위기간 1675~1720) 때 하급관리. 호는 옛 노래란 뜻의 '노가'였고 많은 작품이 전해져 옴.

GIM YUNG He was a general in the reign of King Soog-jong, who ruled from 1675 to 1720. (See poem 60)

김영(金煐) : 숙종(재위기간 1675~1720) 때의 장군.

HAN HO (1543~1605) Han-ho is regarded by many as the greatest calligraphist ever born in this land. In his twenty-fifth year he passed the Preliminary Civil Service Examination, and became a County Magistrate. Dreaming that Wang-heui-ji, the great Chinese calligraphist, handed him a scroll of his own writing, he found himelf, it is said, suddenly endowed with the writing talent. (See poem 11)

한호(韓濩 ; 1543~1605) : 당대의 가장 출중했던 명필가로서 이름이

드높았음. 25세에 초시에 급제하여 지방 관아에서 일함. 중국의 명필가 왕희지에게 친필족자를 선물 받은 꿈을 꾸고 갑자기 붓글씨를 잘 쓰게 되었다고 전해짐.

HWANG JIN I She was a famous dancing girl of Song-do in the days of King Joong-jong who reigned from 1506 to 1544. She is said to have been genteel by birth. (See poem 30, 31)

황진이(黃眞伊) : 중종(재위기간 1506~1544) 때 송도의 이름난 기생. 태생은 양반이었다고 함.

HYO JONG (1619~1659)   Hyo-jong was the 17th king of the I Dynasty. The disgrace of the peace with the Manchus was ever fresh in his memory, and at one time he made preparations in good earnest for a continental expedition of vengeance. In military affairs, he trusted I-wan, and in civil affairs, Song-si-yul was his right hand man. However, he died in his prime and his scheme was abandoned. (See poem 53)

효종(孝宗 ; 1619~1659) : 조선왕조의 17대 왕. 병자호란 때의 치욕적인 평화조약이 기억에 생생하여 한때 대륙정벌을 진지하게 준비한 바 있음. 군사 정무는 이완에게 맡기고 오른팔격인 송시열에게는 민생 정무를 맡겼음. 한창 때에 사망하였고 그에 따라 대륙정벌 계획도 무산됨.

I DUG HYUNG (1561~1613) From his infancy I-dug-hyung showed signs that he was no common mortal. About ten years of age, he began to surprise grown-up people by startling words. In his twentieth year he passed the Civil Service Examination. After that his rise was a quick one. When he was thirty-eight years old, he became one of the Associate Premiers, which was soon followed by premiership. He was humble in spirit, but capable of bravery and fortitude. In private life he was like one hesitating and half-witted. In private life he was like one hesitating and half-witted. But on state occasions of moment he showed plucky decision and grim determination altogether unexpected from his ordinary life. The banishment and doom of his friend I-hang-bog prostrated his spirit that had never failed him for over thirty years through thick and thin. He lost his appetite and called for cold wine till illness ended his life. His pen name was Han-eum. (See poem 34)

이덕형(李德馨 ; 1561~1613) : 어린 시절부터 남다른 소질을 보임. 열 살 무렵, 탁월한 어휘 능력으로 주위 어른들을 놀라게 함. 20세 때 과거 급제하여 이후로 출세가도를 달림. 38세 때는 우의정을 지냈고 이후 영의정에 오름. 인품은 소탈했으나 용감하고 기개가 있다고 전해짐. 개인사에선 조심스럽고 위트도 있는 편이었으나 국정에서는 결단력이 단호했으며 한 치의 양보도 없었다고 함. 친구인 이항복이 유배지로 귀양살이를 하게 되자 30여 년 동안 올곧게 지켜오던 정신이 무너지게 됨. 곡기를 끊고 술만 마시다가 병들어 사망함. 호는 한음(漢陰).

I GAI was the sort of man to hold death at bay by sheer force of will. His emaciated body housed altogether too strong a purpose. He was one of those who might be said to have been born with letters. When he found his uncle frequenting the home of the King's uncle, who later deposed the King, he remonstrated with him. In

1456, caught in a conspiracy against the new ruler with a view to restoring his former lord, he was subjected to tortures till he died. Not a facial muscle of his twitched under he indescribable tortures, it is said. He is one of the Six Martyr Subjects of King Dan-jong. His poem evidently speaks of his devotion to his king.
(See poem 12)

이개(李塏) : 올곧은 강한 절개 때문에 죽음을 맞이함. 몸은 쇠약했으나 의지가 강했음. 문장력이 타고난 사람이었다고 전해짐. 숙부가 왕의 삼촌(후일 단종을 내친 세조)을 자주 방문하자 숙부에게 항의했다고 함. 1456년, 이전 왕의 복귀를 도모하는 역적모의를 가담하였다 하여 고문을 받다가 사망함. 모진 고문에도 얼굴 근육 하나 바뀌지 않았다고 함. 단종의 사육신 중의 한사람. 그의 작품은 단종에 대한 충절의 내용임.

I HANG BOG (1556~1618)   When born, I-hang-bog did not take milk for the first two days, never crying till the fourth day. The frightened family referred the matter to a soothsaying blind man, who prophesied his great future. When only six years old, his father bade him compose a Chines poem on the sword and the harp. He is said to have submitted the following lines at once :

> Manhood is thine, Sword sharp ;
> Ancient note's in the harp.

In his boyhood he was noted for generosity. He often came home without his coat or shoes, giving them away to any boy who was poor enough to be in need of them. He liked to form sham armies and play wild pranks, but, once rebuked by his mother, he devoted his energies to study. He had quick wits and indulged in joking. He seems to have had an exceptionally buoyant spirit for a man of his imposing appearance. He received the title of Prince of O-sung, and his friendship with Han-eum and their joking joustings are of legendary fame and interest. The climax of his official career was when he was made Premier. He was banished to Boog-chung for having remonstrated with the King against his unfilial act to his mother. His poem here was apparently written on his way to the place of banishment, where he soon died. (See pome 33)

이항복(李恒福 ; 1556~1618) : 출생 후 첫 이틀 동안 젖을 먹지 않았고 생후 4일까지 울지도 않아서 이에 놀란 부모가 맹인 점쟁이에게 물어 보자 점쟁이가 장차 아기가 큰 인물이 될 것을 예언했다고 함. 6세 때, 부친이 '칼과 거문고'에 대해 한시를 지으라고 명하자 즉시 다음의 시를 썼다고 함.

예리한 칼은 사내대장부의 기상이요
거문고는 천고의 가락을 지녔도다.

소년시절에는 관대했었다고 전해지는데 옷과 신발을 가난한 소년에게 벗어 주고 자신은 맨발로 귀가한 적도 있었다 함. 병정놀이를 좋아하고 개구쟁이 짓을 심하게 했으나 모친에게 심하게 꾸중을 들은 후 학업에 전념했다고 함. 재치가 있었고 우스갯소리도 잘 했다고 함. 당당한 외모에 쾌활한 성품이었음. 오성부원군이란 칭호도 받았으며 '한음(이덕형)'과의 우정으로 전설적인 일화를 남겨 세간의 이목을

끔. 최고 공직생활은 영의정. 왕이 대비께 불충하자 이에 부당함을 간하다가 북청으로 유배됨. 본서에 실린 작품은 유배지로 귀양 가는 도중에 쓰인 것이며, 유배지에서 곧 사망함.

I HWANG (1501~1570)   I-hwang's place is assured as the greatest ethical philosopher of the sage type the land has ever produced. He stands out for devout simplicity, purity of thought, and intuitive insight. He never liked politics, knowing that it was out of his province. Each time the King called him out of his seclusion to a post of trust, he almost immediately went back to the life of a recluse. He never showed his learning so that it was not until his old age that even his close friends came to recognize a great teacher in him. Then his disciples multiplied. His writings are among the classics most cherished by the people. Some attribute his apathy toward politics to his horrible experience of witnessing his own brother clubbed to death for no other fault than being frank. His pen name was Twe-gye. (See poems 15-20)

이황(李滉 ; 1501~1570) : 이 땅에서 태어난 가장 훌륭한 현학자로 자리매김함. 소박함, 순수함, 통찰력의 소유자로 유명함. 자신의 고장을 떠나기 싫어 정치에 입문하기를 꺼려했음. 왕이 관직을 주기 위해 부를 때마다 칩거생활로 들어감. 자신의 학문을 절대로 남에게 보여주지 않아서 가까운 친구들조차 그가 노령이 되어서야 그 가치를 알게 되었다고 함. 이후 학자의 학문을 배우고자 학생들이 몰려듦. 그의 작품들은 사람들이 고이 간직하는 명작 중의 명작이 됨. 그가 정치에 냉담했던 이유는 형이 솔직했다는 어이없는 이유로 맞아 죽었기 때문임. 호는 퇴계(退溪).

I JOONG JIB   Nothing is known of him. Even his name is in dispute. Some call him I-joong-nag. (See poems 72)

이중집(李仲集) : 그에 대한 기록이 별로 없으며 이름조차 확실치 않음. 작가를 '이중락'이라고 하는 사람들도 있음.

I JUNG BO   Nothing is known of him except that he was Grand Master of Learning in the days of King Yung-jo who reigned from 1725 to 1776. (See poems 61)

이정보(李鼎輔) : 영조(재위기간 1725~1776) 때 대제학을 지냈으며 그 밖엔 알려진 바 없음.

 I JUNG SIN   Nothing is known of him except that he had Jib joong for his pen name, and Baig-hoi-dang was what his intimate friends called him. (See poems 65-67)

이정신(李廷藎) : 자는 집중(集中)이었고 친우들은 백회재(百悔齋)이라 부름. 그 밖엔 알려진 바 없음.

I MYUNG HAN (1595~1645)   I-myung-han passed the preliminary and final C. S. Examination in his sixteenth and twenty-second year respectively. Finally he rose to be Grand Master of Learning succeeding his father and later to be succeeded by his own son — a thing held altogether unusual. He was taken to Mukdon, then called Simyang, to answer for his opposition to peace during the Manchu Invasion but later released. (See poem 49~51)

이명한(李明漢 ; 1595~1645) : 16세 때 초시에 급제하고 22세 때 전시에 급제함. 부친에 이어 대제학을 지냈으며 후일 아들에게 물려줌. 이

는 흔치 않은 일이었음. 병자호란 때 청과 맺은 조약에 반대하여 묵뎬
(그 당시 심양으로 불렸음)으로 압송되었으나 후일 풀려남.

I SOON SIN (1545~1598) Any one who reads the life of I-soon-sin can not but be reminded of the English Nelson. To all appearance, he seems to have had a headstrong, intractable even mischievous boyhood. Everyone, it is said, was in fear of his wild pranks. Little could have been expected from such a wayward youth of the hearty, sterling manhood he developed later in life. He invented the famous "tortoise boat", the first ironclad, and routed the Hideyoshi fleets. He fell in the last decisive sea battle, the greatest ever known in the history of the land. Ordering his adjutants to keep his death secret till the fight was over, he passed away peacefully, happy with the knowledge that he had won the day. In his early days he once refused a high officer's offer of his daughter's hand for the reason that it would smack of seeking favor through marriage. He was at once revered and loved by his men, and the news of his death plunged the whole nation into deep mourning. (See poem 29)

이순신(李舜臣 ; 1545~1598) : 이순신의 생애를 읽은 사람은 누구나 영국의 넬슨제독을 떠올리게 됨. 어느 모로 보나 이순신은 고집불통 개구쟁이 유년시절을 보냈던 것으로 보임. 모두가 그의 고약한 장난을 두려워했다고 함. 개구쟁이 유년시절에서 후일 멀쩡한 성인이 되리라고도 누구도 예상치 못했다고 함. 그 유명한 국내 최초의 철갑선인 "거북선"을 만들어 일본의 히데요시 함대를 무찌르기도 함. 국내 역사상 가장 유명했던 해전에서 쓰러졌을 때 전투가 끝나기까지 자신의 죽음을 비밀로 하라는 명을 남기고 임종했음. 전투에 이겼음을 알

고 행복해하며 평화로이 생을 마감한 것임. 한때 고위관직을 권하는 딸의 요청을 거절한 바 있음. 이유는 출가외인의 손을 빌려 이득을 본다는 오해를 받기 싫어서임. 이순신은 부하들에게 존경과 사랑을 받았고 그의 사망 소식이 전해지자 온 국민이 애통해 함.

I WUN IG (1547~1634)   I-wun-ig's pen name was O-ri. Whatever the fact was, his shortness of stature ia still proverbial. He was a mild, calm, confidence-inspiring sort of man with an unimpeachable record of private life. He served three successive kings, but no one ever thought, or at least spoke, ill of him. After the deposition of Gwang-hai-jo, the lewd, lawless prince, people were in an uneasy state of suspense, wondering what O-ri had to say. At his appearance in the city on his way to see the new King, they congratulated one another, saying, "Peace, peace to all. Premier O-ri is come." When he at last resigned for age, King In-jo conferred on him plain cotton quilts in remembrance of his self-denying services for the country. From the officicial despatched to see him to his country home, the King learned on inquiry that stars could be seen through his thatched roof and his walls were not windtight. "What!" exclaimed the King, "hasn't he got a decent house after forty years of high official life?" The Provincial Governor was immediately ordered to build him a house befitting his station. After his death, nothing was left to bury him with. The King sent the Crown Prince and the Chamberlain with money to see him duly buried. The whole nation cried over his death as in personal bereavement. Perhaps his poem here was the good-bye he was bidding to his departing lord whose tyrannic rule the people could no longer endure. It was cloaked in the appearance of a love song, for it was highly dangerous to show any sort of attachment to the deposed king. (See poem 32)

이원익(李元翼 ; 1547~1634) : 호는 오리(梧里). 키가 작았다고 전해지며 온화하고 침착하며 고무적인 성품이었고 사생활도 나무랄 데가 없었다고 함. 생전에 왕을 세 분 모셨는데 어느 누구도 이원익을 나쁘게 보지 않았다고 함. 광해군이 방탕하고 무법적이어서 폐위당한 후 사람들은 불안감에 휩싸여 이원익이 무슨 말을 할까 궁금해 함. 그래서 이원익이 새 왕을 알현하러 가는 길에 마을에 모습을 드러내자 사람들이 서로를 경축하며 "조용, 조용히 하시오, 모두들. 영의정께서 오셨소이다."라고 외쳤음. 이후 연로하여 정계를 떠날 때 인조가 솜이불을 하사하여 나라에 봉직한 노고를 치하함. 이원익의 시골 생활이 궁금하여 왕이 사람을 보냈는데 초가지붕 사이로 별이 보이고 벽에서는 바람이 숭숭 나오더란 보고를 받자 왕이 황망하여 "40년 고위관직 에 어찌 멀쩡한 집 한 채가 없는고?"하며 지방 사또를 즉시 보내 그에 걸맞는 집을 지어주었다고 함. 사후에는 함께 땅에 묻어줄 물품조차 없었다고 함. 이에 왕이 세자와 신료들을 보내 후히 장사 치르라 명함. 온 백성은 자신의 육친이 죽은 듯 그의 죽음을 애통해 했다고 함. 본서에 실린 시는 떠나는 군주에게 안녕을 고하는 작품인데 이 군주는 폭정을 가하여 백성들이 도저히 견딜 수가 없어 폐위된 것이기에 폐위된 왕에게 애착을 보이는 것은 위험했으므로 연애시로 보이게끔 지어진 것임.

JO CHAN HAN In 1601 Jo-chan-han passed the preliminary Civil Service Examination. Six years later he also succeeded in passing the final test. He is credited with the exploits of exterminating the gangs of bandits which sere laying waste a part of South Korea. (See poem 52)

조찬한(趙纘韓) : 1601년, 초시에 급제. 6년 뒤에는 전시에 급제함. 남쪽 지방을 황폐케 하는 산적들을 소탕하는 공적을 쌓기도 함.

JO HUN (1544~1592)   Jo-hun seems to have had an upright mind and an iron purpose, a character at once sweet and heroic. He and his seven hundred men, all volunteers, felt like a man at Geum-san in the Hideyoshi Invasion. When he was only four years old, while reading his lesson under a tree in company with other boys, a passing dignitary and his retinue made a halt near them. All the other children ran toward the party and peeped at them from curiosity, but Jo reminded reading unmoved. The prominent person beckoned to him and asked the reason. The child answered kneeling, "It is my father's order, sir, to attend to my studies." After his death, niche was made for him in the National Shrine of Confucius by a royal decree. (See poem 27, 28)

조헌(趙憲 ; 1544~1592) : 올곧은 기개와 강건한 결의를 가진 성품인데 부드러우면서도 용감했던 것으로 보임. 일본의 히데요시가 침략해 왔을 때 금산에서 700명의 의병과 한몸이 되어 싸움. 그가 4세 때의 일화가 있음. 나무 밑에서 아이들과 공부를 하고 있는데 한 고관이 시종을 거느리고 그 옆을 지나가다가 멈추었다고 함. 모든 아이들이 호기심에서 그 일행을 향해 뛰어갔지만 조헌은 미동도 않은 채 독서에 열중했다고 함. 고관은 조헌을 불러 연유를 물으니 소년은 무릎을 꿇고 대답하기를 "제 부친께서 학업에 전념하라 명했나이다." 그가 사망하자 왕명으로 공자 사당에 그의 명패가 올랐음.

JOO EUI SIG was a County Governor and noted singer in the reign of King Soog-jong who ruled from 1675 to 1720. (See poem 39)
주의식(朱義植) : 숙종(재위기간 1675~1720) 때 지방관아의 우두머리였으며 노래에 탁월한 소질이 있었음.

JUNG CHOONG SIN (1576~1636) Jung-choong-sin started life from obscure origin, and, by steadiness coupled with ingenuity, rose to the rank of Vice Marshal. Hideyoshi's army invaded the land. Bows and arrows against firelocks, there was no resisting their onrush. Yet volunteers flocked to wherever the appeal was made by an influential person. It was thus that Jung, then scarcely a lad, joined one of the volunteer groups. Gwun-ryool, the volunteer leader, wanted to dispatch a messenger to the King who had removed to the north and was more than a thousand ri away. The road was beset with dangers. Jung, then only seventeen years old, volunteered to go. It proved the beginning of his fortune. I-hang-bog, the War Minister, got interested in the spirited messenger-boy, gave him education, and opened a career for him. Jung rendered the country great services by putting down many serious rebellions.
(See poem 38)
정충신(鄭忠信 ; 1576~1636) : 출신 신분은 낮았으나 훌륭한 솜씨와 절개가 굳어 포도대장 벼슬까지 오름. 히데요시가 침략해 왔을 때 활과 화살로는 일본의 소총을 당해낼 재간이 없었지만 의병들이 곳곳에서 모여들었고 정충신도 이때 의병에 지원했는데 겨우 소년티를 벗어

난 나이였음. 당시 의병장이었던 권율이 왕에게 밀사를 보내고자 했는데 이때 왕은 북방에 피신 차 가있었는데 천리 길이었음. 길은 곳곳에 위험이 도사리고 있었지만 정충신은 겨우 17세의 나이에 이를 지원하고 나섬. 이후 그의 운명이 새로이 시작됨. 당시 일본과의 전투를 관장하던 이항복은 정충신의 기백에 관심을 가져 그를 교육시키고 출세의 길을 열어줌. 이후 반란군을 진압 하는 등 나라에 큰 공을 세움.

JUNG CHUL (1536~1593) In 1562 Jung-chul passed the civil Service Examination with the highest honours. In 1589 he became Left Associate Premier, and two years later was wrongfully banished to Gang-gye. He must have had an impressive appearance, for someone who had met him in the midst of privations and hardships still wrote of him as a "celestial being." He was square in dealing and outspoken to the degree of intolerance. Numerous songs are attributed to him. (See poems 24-26)

정철(鄭澈 ; 1536~1593) : 1562년, 좋은 성적으로 과거시험에 합격. 1589년, 좌의정으로 봉직했고 2년 뒤에 강계로 귀양 감. 어렵게 살 때 그를 만났던 사람이 그를 '천사'로 표현한 걸 보면 남다른 면모를 가졌던 걸로 보임. 매사에 공징했으며 지나칠 정도로 솔직했으며 많은 작품을 남김.

JUNG MONG JOO (1337~1392)   A martyr-subject of the Go-ryu Dynasty, Jung-mong-joo is a living presence, enshrined in the hearts of the people. He stands for manhood and loyalty. He did not turn his back on a losing cause, dying for it in the end. He saw that things were going wrong, I-sung-gye, the founder of the I Dynasty, rising daily in power. At a banquet, I's son, who later assumed the royal title of Tai-jong improvised a poem hinting that Jung would gain by going over to his side. The poem here given was a sort of refusal sung back. At that time he held a post of trust. Shortly afterward he paid a visit to I-sung-gye ostensibly on the pretext of inquiring after his health but really to sound him out, and there he knew that his end was near at hand. On his way home he repeatedly ordered his servant to leave him, who repeatedly refused to obey. They met their death at the Sun-joog-gyo Bridge, embracing each other. Even to this day, the stone bridge is held to retain the blood stains. (See poem 2)

정몽주(鄭夢周 ; 1337~1392) : 고려 왕조의 충신으로 사람들의 마음속에 소중히 간직되어 있음. 사나이다움과 충절로 알려졌으며 죽는 한이 있어도 대의에 어긋나는 것을 하지 않음. 조선왕조를 세운 이성계가 매일 힘을 키워가는 것을 보고 사태의 심각성을 깨달음. 이성계의 아들(훗날 태종이 됨)이 연회에서 정몽주에게 시를 건넴. 내용은 이성계 쪽으로 유인하는 시인데 본서에 실린 작품은 거절의 내용을 담고 있는 화답시 형태임. 그 당시 정몽주는 주요 직위에 있었음. 얼마 안 있어 이성계의 문병을 핑계로 이성계를 방문하지만 실상은 그를 타진해보기 위함이었음. 그러나 이 방문 때 자신의 죽음이 임박했음을 눈치 챘고 귀가하는 도중에 동행하던 하인에게 자신을 두고 어서 도망가라고 종용했으나 하인이 이를 거부함. 결국 두 사람은 서로를 부둥켜 앉은 채 선죽교에서 피살됨. 오늘날까지도 선죽교에는 혈흔이 남아 있다고 함.

JUNG MONG JOO'S MOTHER The poem is often falsely credited to Jung-mong-joo, but it is really his mother's, a woman of sterling virtues, for aught we know. Her family name was I. Jung must have owed much of what he was to her good influence. She used to make him blue clothes with scarlet lining. By way of explanation she said that a boy should grow to be a man with a suave appearance but a burning heart. (See poem 3)

정몽주 모친 : 정몽주 모친의 시가 정몽주의 시로 오인된 바가 종종 있는데 작품 내용은 여성의 덕목에 관한 것으로 보임. 모친의 성씨는 이씨였으며 정몽주가 모친의 영향력을 많이 받아 거목이 되었다함. 모친은 정몽주의 옷을 파란색으로 만들어 입혔으며 안감은 붉은색이었는데 그 뜻은 외모는 점잖되 마음은 강렬하게 자라라는 당부였다고 함.

JUNG TAI HWA (1602~1673) In the year 1628, Jung-tai-hwa passed the Civil Service Examination. During the Manchu Invasion, he was Secretary to the Commander-in chief. When the host of mounted Manchu soldiers came in sight, the commander-in-chief took to flight, leaving his army doing the same panic-stricken. Jung rose to the moment, rallied the scattered men and put up such a terrific resistance that the enemy beat a retreat. His sagacity proved by this and other incidents, he was made Premier in the end. (See poem 54)

정태화(鄭太和 ; 1602~1673) : 1628년, 과거 급제함. 병자호란 때 도원수를 모시고 있었는데 청나라 군사들이 떼로 몰려오자 총 우두머리 도원수가 도망을 감. 이에 병사들이 갈피를 못 잡아 우왕좌왕했는데 이때 정태화가 홀연히 봉기하여 흩어진 군사를 모으고 결사 항전하여 적이 퇴각함. 이런저런 사건을 영민하게 잘 처리하여 후일 영의정에 오름.

MYUNG OG　Nothing is known of her except that she was a famous dancing girl of Soo-wun, the called Hwa-sung. (see poem 70)
명옥(明玉) : 수원(당시는 화성이라 불림)의 유명한 기생. 그 외 알려진 바 없음.

NAM GOO MAN (1628~1711)　Nam-goo-man successfully passed the Civil Service Examination. While he was Governor of Ham-gyung Province, he sent to the King maps he had made of the borderland, urging the necessity of establishing Moo-san as a strategic border town. He was made Minister of Justice, but, for impeaching some influential personages on no sufficient grounds, he was banished. Soon he was pardoned and resumed the official career. He finally became Premier. (See poem 57)
남구만(南九萬 ; 1628~1711) : 과거시험에서 우수한 성적으로 합격함. 함경도 지방의 우두머리로 있을 때, 국경지역을 그린 지도를 왕에게 바치고 '무산'을 전략기지화 할 필요가 있음을 주청드림. 형조판서가 되었지만 충분한 근거도 없이 고관대작을 탄핵했다고 하여 귀양을 감. 곧 방면되어 다시 공직에 오르고 후일 영의정이 됨.

OO TAG (1252~1342) Oo-tag began his official career by passing the Civil Service Examination, and became Master of Ceremonies. He was a fearless, straightforward character. Once he brought a written remonstrance against the King's misconduct, which the counsellors dared not read to him. Then and there he denounced them all, shouting that they were responsible for the King's shameful deed. He seems to have been profoundly learned and penetrating. When the "Jung-jun", a commentary on the "Joo-yug", the most recondite writing of Confucius, made its way into the land, it was he who confined himself with it for a month and came out with all the explanations ever possible. (See poem 1)

우탁(禹倬 ; 1252~1342) : 과거 급제하여 공직생활을 시작했고 성균제주(成均祭酒)가 됨. 성품은 대담무쌍했고 올곧았음. 한번은 왕의 실책을 바로잡는 글을 올렸는데 신하들이 감히 왕에게 읽어드릴 수가 없었다고 함. 그러자 그 자리에서 왕의 그릇된 행동은 대신들의 책임이 크다고 소리치며 대신들을 비난했다고 함. 학문이 깊었고 통찰력이 있었던 걸로 보임. '주역'(공자가 쓴 가장 난해한 책)의 주해서인 '정전'이 국내에 들어오자 한 달 동안 칩거하여 그 책을 모두 풀이한 해설서를 내놓았다고 함.

SIN HEUI MOON Nothing is known of him except that he was also called Myung-yoo by his intimate friends. (See poems 68, 69)

신희문(申喜文) : 벗들이 명유(明裕)라 불렀고 그 외에 알려진 바 없음.

SIN HEUM (1566~1628) A man of brilliant gifts and ready wit, Sin-heum had an illustrious career. He became Prime Minister towards the close of his life. (See poems 35,36)

신흠(申欽 ; 1566~1628) : 재주가 출중했고 재치가 있었으며 활약이 눈부셨다고 함. 말년엔 영의정을 지냄.

SONG JONG WUN   He had Goon-sung for his current name. Noting more is known of him. (See poem 64)

송종원(宋宗元) : 당대에는 군성(君星)이란 이름이었다고 함. 그 외에 알려진 바 없음.

SONG SI YUL (1607~1689)   It is said that just before Song-si-yul's birth his father dreamed Confucius coming to his home. He early devoted himself to the classics, especially to the writing of Joo-ja, the great Chinese commentator on the books of Confucius. He passed the Civil Service Examination leading the list. He followed the royal party to Nam-han-san-sung during the Manchu Invasion, whence he issued lamenting over the shameful peace treaty, bidding Final goodbye to his court life. However, when King Hyo-jong who was seriously contemplating a war with the Manchus, called him by a letter of his own writing, Song came back with a resolution to do all he could for the cause. The King died in the midst of warlike preparations, and the whole scheme crumbled to the ground. He rose to the position of Left Associate Premier under the young monarch, devoting himself to the moral education of the people by upholding Confucianism. Meanwhile a political feud raged, the nucleus of the so-called "Four Colours", four political clans different in no platform but united in bloody nepotism. He fell victim to the feud as the leader of one of the clans. He was first banished and later decreed to drink a venom and die. While in power, he was a dread to his foes, a sage to his own followers. On the night of his execution, it is said, a bright star was seen to fall from the eastern sky and a milky-way-like sheen stood from earth to heaven. He wrote numerous books. To be justly appreciated, he has still to be disentangled from the mass of fierce, jarring cavilling and counter-cavilling. His pen name was Oo-am. (See poem 56)

송시열(宋時烈 ; 1607~1689) : 송시열이 태어나기 직전 부친의 꿈에 공자가 나타나 집으로 들어왔다고 함. 그래서인지 일찌감치 어린나이에 고전, 특히 주자(공자가 쓴 책에다 주해를 단 중국의 대학자)의 글에 심취했고 과거에 장원급제함. 병자호란 때는 왕과 고관대작을 따라 남한산성으로 피신함. 그때 체결된 평화조약에 수치심을 느껴 한탄하다가 벼슬을 버리고 궁궐을 떠남. 그러나 병자호란을 통탄해 하는 효종이 친필로 그를 대궐로 부르자 대의명분을 위해 굳은 결심을 하고 다시 대궐로 입성함. 전시체제의 준비를 하는 도중에 왕이 죽게 되자 모든 계획은 수포로 돌아가고 그 후 좌의정 반열에 올라 어린 왕을 보필했음. 이때 백성들에게 유교를 숭상하게 하여 윤리교육에 매진함. 그 동안 사색 당파싸움이 격렬해지자 당쟁에 휘말려 우두머리인 까닭에 희생양이 됨. 귀양 갔으나 유배지에서 사약을 받고 사망함. 권력을 잡고 있을 때 적에게는 냉엄했고 자신의 추종자에게는 어질었다고 함. 사약을 받는 날 밤에는 밝은 별 하나가 동쪽 하늘에서 떨어졌다고 하며 은하수 같은 광채가 땅에서 하늘로 뻗어 있었다고 함. 수많은 저서를 남겼는데 이젠 트집 잡으면서 신랄하게 치고받는 알력 싸움에서 벗어나 그에 대한 정당한 평가가 이루어져야 함. 호는 우암(尤菴).

SONG SOON (1493~1583) When Song-soon was Vice Home minister, he made a point of recommending to the Throne only men of worth, irrespective of their birth or connections. This earned him enmity of some influential persons, which ended in his banishment lasting five years. His bastard uncle once remarked that he had seen no high official come out of South Gate, all leaving Seoul by West Small Gate (admitting the passage of corpses), hinting that no one was willing to leave power and honour until it was too late. Meeting his uncle after his retirement, he said jokingly, "Now I have come out of South Gate." (See poem 10)

송순(宋純 ; 1493~1583) : 이조참판이었을 때 출생이나 친인척과 상관 없이 우수한 자가 왕좌에 올라야 한다는 논설을 펴 이에 높은 분들의 적개심을 사서 5년 동안 귀양길에 오름. 한번은 숙부가 이르기를 고관대작은 남대문으로 나오지 않고 모두들 서대문(시신을 통과시켜 주는 문)으로 한성을 떠나더라고 했음. 이는 권력과 영광은 한 번 잡으면 쉽게 놓지를 못해 결국 너무 늦도록 퇴임을 않는다는 뜻임. 이에 송순은 일찍이 사퇴하여 삼촌을 만나 우스개 삼아 말하기를 "저는 남대문으로 나왔습니다."

SU GYUNG DUG (1489~1546)   Born in a poverty-stricken home but highly gifted, Su-gyung-dug managed to learn by himself. By his father's command he sat for the Preliminary Civil Service Examination and succeeded in passing it, but, having a philosophical turn of mind, soon took to a secluded life. He built himself a cottage by a rock-bedded pool called Hwa-dam near the city of Song-do, and there devoted himself to meditation and reading. He always firstturned problem over in his mind for days or even for weeks till clear ideas crystallized before he referred it to books. Enraptured with abstract researches he thought nothing of worldly things. Having feasted in his cheery conversation until past noon a certain Song, one of his pupils , chanced to find through the cookthat he hadtasted nothing for two days.He was appointed to a government position, but, poor as he was, he declined the offer.(See pome 14)

서경덕(徐敬德 ; 1489~1546) : 가난한 집에서 태어났으나 재능이 높아 독학했음. 부친의 명령으로 초시에 급제하였으나 철학적인 사상을 갖고 은둔생활로 접어듦. 송도 옆 '화담'이란 돌 웅덩이 옆에 작은 오두막집을 짓고 명상을 하며 외부세계와 단절함. 문제가 생기면 마음속에 몇 날 몇 주 고민하다가 명쾌히 해결되면 책에다 적음. 추상적인 것에 매료되어 세상적인 일에는 생각도 하지 않음. 송씨 성을 가진 제자가 말하기를 스승은 12시까지 재미있는 대화에 빠지기도 하고 이틀 동안 아무것도 입에 대지 않은 적도 있었다고 함. 이는 밥해주는 사람을 통해 들었다고 함. 관직에 제의도 받았으나 사는 형편이 넉넉지 않았는데도 그 제의를 거절함.

SUNG HON (1535~1598)   When Sung-hon was scarcely twelve years old, he could read difficult classics with such an understanding that he became and object of wonder. He failed to sit for the Civil Service Examinations on account of illness. I-yool-gog, the great scholar-politician, seems to have given him a lift. He became one of the Royal Counsellors. When his friend was gone, he also retired. Thenceforward he lived in seclusion as a weighty scholar of much following. During the Hideyoshi Invasion, however, he was deprived of his official titles, partly because he failed to meet the King, who was then moving north to seek safety, although the route lay close by his home, and partly through his advocation of peace. But he was soon restored to his full official dignity. (See poem 23)

성혼(成渾 ; 1535~1598) : 12세도 채 되기 전에 어려운 고전을 읽을 수 있어서 선망의 대상이 됨. 과거 날에 병이 나 시험에 임할 수 없었으나 이율곡(학자이자 정치가)이 출세의 길을 열어주어 훗날 왕의 측근에서 중요관직 맡아 일함. 친구가 퇴임했을 때는 따라 퇴임함. 이후 줄곧 은둔생활을 했으며 위대한 학자로 따르는 이가 많았음. 히데요시가 침입했을 때는 왕을 배알할 수가 없어 관직을 빼앗김. 당시 왕은 북쪽으로 피난 중이었는데 왕의 행차길이 그의 집 바로 옆이었지만 왕을 만나보지 못했음. 이때 그는 평화를 주창하고 나섰기 때문임. 이후 곧 관직에 복귀됨.

SUNG SAM MOON (1418~1456) There is a story that Sung-sam-moon derived his name from the fact that just before his birth a voice in the air thrice asked whether he had been born, sam-moon meaning "questioning three times." When Sye-jo deposed the young king, his nephew, to accede to the throne himself. Sung hatched a plot to restore his rightful lord, while feigning submission and retaining his post. He was betrayed on the eve of action, and executed with his father and three brothers. He is one of the famous Six Martyr Subjects. He was a joking, easy-going sort of man, with no prepossessing appearance. But as events proved, he was a man of fortitude and inflexible will. (See poem 7)

성삼문(成三問 ; 1418~1456) : 그의 이름에 대한 유래가 있음. 그가 출생 전 하늘에서 출생 여부를 묻는 질문이 3번 있었다 하여 삼문(三問)이 되었다 함. 세조가 조카인 어린 왕을 내쫓고 왕이 되자, 굴복하는 척하며 관직을 지키다가 옛 왕을 복귀시키려고 음모를 꾸밈. 그러나 바로 전날 밤 모반자가 있어 반역이 탄로나게 되어 부친 및 형제 3명과 사형당하여 사육신 중에 한명이 됨. 성품이 명랑하고 느긋했고 외모는 별로 호감형이 아니었음. 여러 면에서 입증되었듯이 꿋꿋한 사람이었고 불굴의 의지를 소유했음.

WUL SAN DAI GOON He was the eldest son of King Dug-jong, receiving the title of dai-goon, Grand Prince, in 1491. He had a pure mind and an unusual love for letters. He did not like pomp and display. He himself wrote beautifully. He is credited with several volumes of poetry. King Sung-jong used to visit his home privately, with no royal retinue. (See poem 9)

월산대군(月山大君) : 1497년 덕종(세조의 아들로 세자였으나 즉위 전에 병으로 죽음)의 맏아들로 성종의 친형. 성품이 순수하고 남달리 문학에 대해 애착을 가졌다고 함. 화려함과 겉치레를 싫어했음. 아름다운 작품을 썼고 시집 여러 권을 내어 능력을 인정받음. 성종이 수행원을 대동하지 않고 그의 집을 자주 방문했다고 함.

WUN CHUN SUG The misrule of the closing days of the Go-ryu Dynasty early decided him to lead a secluded life. Tai-jong, the third king of the I Dynasty, in his youth, studied Chinese classics under Wun. On his way to the Diamond Mountains, the King called a halt near his former master's home and asked him for an interview. He purposely went out and did not see the King, who, it is said, only gave his left-over food to his maidservant and proceeded on his journey. He wrote history and, locking up the manuscript in a box, inscribed on it to the effect that no posterity, if not quite worthy of him, should open it. In the days of his grandchildren, the family consulted together and decided to open the box, now that those whom the writings might have hurt had all passed away. On opening, they found a history clashing in many important points with the one in the royal archives. Fearing that the thing might take wind and bring ruin to the family, they dertroyed it. (See poem 4)

원천석(元天錫) : 고려 왕조 말엽 은둔생활에 접어듦. 조선왕조의 3번째 왕인 태종이 어렸을 때 원천석에게 중국 고전을 사사 받음. 태종이 금강산 가는 길에 스승이었던 그를 만나보고자 집 근처에 멈춰 만나기를 청하자 고의로 집을 나가 버렸으며 왕을 만나지 않음. 이에 왕은 여자 가복에게 음식을 하사하고 행차를 계속했다고 전해짐. 원천석은 역사를 써서 상자에 넣어 자물쇠로 채웠으며 상자에 글씨를 새겨 후손이 함부로 열지 않도록 했음. 그러나 손자 세대에 내려와 가족이 상의하여 상자를 열어보기로 함. 왜냐하면 글에 적힌 내용 때문에 다치게 될 수 있는 사람들은 이미 세상을 하직했기 때문임. 상자를 열어보니 역사적 내용이 왕의 서가에 있는 중요 내용들과 다름을 발견함. 그래서 혹시 한 차례 풍파가 일어나 가족에게 해가 미칠까 두려워 파기시켜 버렸다고 함.

WUN HO In 1423 Wun-ho passed the Civil Service Examination. When he saw King Dan-jong's uncle grow in power, he retired from the official life for good. When Dan-jong was dethroned and banished to Yung-wul, the most mountainous county, he followed his unhappy lord. He built a hur by a stream which perhaps was flowing past both his dwelling and his lord's. Of course, there was no communicating between them. There he wept morning and evening till the deposed king died. He came home after the three mourning years had passed. He always refused to see any official. Once a relative of his, who was a Provincial Governor, came in plain clothes and asked to see him. The moment he came out and saw who it really was, he turned on his heel without a word. He is said to have removed into the mountains to stand no risk of coming across an official. Before his death he burned up all his manuscripts, enjoining his posterity not to learn letters. King Soong-jong conferred the Loyalty Gate on his surviving family. He was one of he famous Six Living Subjects of King Dan-jong. (See poem 13)

원호(元昊) : 1423년, 과거 급제함. 단종의 숙부가 권력을 잡는 것을 보고 공직생활을 영원히 떠남. 단종이 폐위되어 첩첩산골 영월로 위리안치 될 때 따라감. 그는 개울가에 오막살이 집 한 채를 짓고 살았는데 그 개울물은 원호의 집과 단종의 집을 지나쳐서 흐르는 것으로 추정되지만 두 사람은 대화를 할 수가 없었음. 그곳에 살면서 원호는 밤낮을 눈물로 지냈으며 결국 왕은 세상을 떠남. 3년 상을 마치고 집에 돌아와서는 어떤 공직자도 만나지 않았다고 함. 한 번은 지방관아에 벼슬을 하는 친척 한 명이 소탈한 옷차림으로 와 만나기를 청했지만 그를 보자 말 한마디 건네지 않고 뒤 돌아섰다고 함. 오다가다 공직자를 만날까봐 산중으로 들어가 살았다고 함. 자신이 죽기 전에 모든 기록들을 불태우고 후손들이 학문을 배우지 않기를 명함. 숙종 때 그의 가문에 정려문을 하사하여 충정을 칭송함. 단종의 생육신 중에 한 사람으로 남음.

YANG SA EUN (1517~1584) Yang-sa-eun was a calligraphist whose fame has grown into a legend. He is said to have been especially good at writing big characters. Once he made a gigantic Chinese character meaning "to fly", and ordered that it be guarded jealously, for he had put his life into it. His son kept it locked in a closet. One day a sudden gale arose from the sea, swept it out of the room, and bore it away skyward. The legend adds that this happened on the anniversary of his death. To all appearance, his official career was no distinguished one. (See poem 22)

양사언(楊士彦 ; 1517~1584) : 명성이 전설이 될 정도로 위대한 문필가였으며 특히 큰 글씨체를 잘 썼다고 함. 한 번은 '날다'의 뜻인 한문을 크게 쓰고 그 글씨에 생명을 불어 넣었으니 잘 보관하라고 명했음. 아들은 그 글씨를 벽장에 넣어 열쇠를 채웠음. 그러나 어느 날 갑자기 바다에서 돌풍이 생기더니 방에 들어와 그 글씨를 휩쓸고 나와 하늘 높이 가져가 버림. 그때가 우연히 양사언의 기일이었다고 함. 공직생활로는 이렇다 할 것을 남기지 않음.

YOON SUN DO (1587~1671) Thanks to his sharp tongue and fearless spirit, he spent his heyday of life in banishment covering twenty years upwards altogether. In his written appeals to the throne he denounced influential persons, including state ministers,for their evil-doings, The bitter experience of banishment never daunted his spirit. He was ever ready to be banished, never willing to compromise the rigour of his straight language. However, at intervals the court recognized his merit, and called him back to service. The climax of his official career was reached when he was made Counsellor on

Ceremonies. One long series of descriptive songs has earned him the unchallenged position as the most lyrical "si-jo" writer.
(See poems 47, 48)

윤선도(尹善道 ; 1587~1671) : 신랄한 언변과 두려움 없는 기백 때문에, 한창 젊을 때 20년간 유배 생활을 함. 상소문을 올려 재상들을 포함한 고위 관직자들의 악행을 비난함. 힘든 유배생활도 그의 기백을 꺾지 못했고 기꺼이 귀양 갈 각오로 혹독하게 직언을 했다고 함. 하지만 가끔씩 조정에서는 그의 장점을 인정하여 공직에 불러들이기도 함. 그의 공직생활의 전성기는 예조참의 때임. 여러 연으로 된 긴 시를 썼으며 가장 서정적인 시조작가라는 이름을 얻음.

SONGS FROM KOREA

해 설

변영태 영역시조의 아름다움

조규익

(숭실대 교수/한국문예연구소 소장)

들어가는 말

'번역은 반역'이라지만,[1] 다른 언어 사용자들에게 '내 글로 만든' 문학작품이나 담론들을 읽히기 위해서는 번역이라는 수단을 활용할 수밖에 없다. 문학작품의 번역에는 단순한 축어(逐語)나 축자(逐字) 수준의 '말 바꾸기'를 넘어 의식이나 사상 혹은 담론 자체의 치환으로 상승되지 못하는 한계가 늘 문제로 지적되어 왔다. 공감하기 쉬운 '지금 이 순간'의 언술들이 아니라 통시적·공시적 징표들을 고루 갖춘 문학적 담론들일수록 번역이 힘든 것도 그런 까닭이다. 쉽지는 않겠지만, '동적[dynamic]인 번역, 정확성·명확성과 자연스러움을 갖춘

---

1 박상익, 『번역은 반역인가』, 도서출판 푸른역사, 2006, 7~11쪽 참조.

번역, 의미·형태·기분·문체 등이 제대로 전달되게 하는 번역'2 만이 잘 된 번역일 수 있다는 지적이 타당한 것도 그 때문이다.

그런 점에서 수백 년을 내려오며 시대 조류의 변이(變移)나 인정(人情)의 기미(幾微)를 반영하게 된 민족 고유의 노랫말인 시조의 번역이야말로 그리 수월한 일은 아니다.3 그럼에도 불구하고 이른 시기부터 지금까지 시조를 한문, 일문(日文), 영문 등으로 꾸준히 번역해 오고 있는 것은 그것이 우리 민족의 심성 영역을 잘 표현하는 장르라고 보았기 때문일 것이다.

현재까지 이 분야의 첫 시도로 생각되는 변영태4의 영역(英譯) 시조를 대상으로 그 특징과 의미를 분석해 보려는 것이 본고의 의도다. 그는 시조·현대시·동화 등 여러 장르들을 영어로 번역했는데,5 그

---

2 박진임, 「한국문학의 세계화와 번역의 문제 : 시조의 영어 번역을 중심으로」, 『번역학 연구』 제8권 1호[2007년 봄], 한국번역학회, 2007, 154쪽.

3 물론 '시조는 간결하고 정제된 문학 양식이며 서경과 서정의 결합이 유기적으로 이루어져 있어 번역 텍스트에서도 원텍스트의 미학이 상당히 많이 유지된다는 장점을 지닌다. 즉 간결한 형식 자체가 번역을 용이하게 할뿐더러 그 형식 속에 전개되는 풍부한 이미지와 의미 또한 용이하게 번역될 때가 많다'[박진임, 같은 논문, 156쪽]는 견해도 있지만, '산문보다는 운문 쪽이 불가능에 가까울 만큼 힘든 작업으로서 시 번역은 창작에 버금가는 문학 작업'[윤종혁, 「文學作品 飜譯의 可能性 與否에 關하여」, 『Veritas』 6, 명지대학교 영어영문학과, 1989, 115쪽]이라는 견해가 더 타당하다. 서술적 어조의 산문과 달리 시대를 달리 하는 압축적 운문인 고시조를 외국의 현대 독자들이 이해할 수 있도록 번역하는 일이 그리 수월한 일일 수는 없는 것도 그 때문이다.

4 변영태(1892~1969). 정치가이자 영문학자이며, 본관은 밀양, 호는 일석(逸石). 19세에 보성중학교 졸업 후 만주에 가서 통화현(通化縣)의 신흥학교를 1회로 졸업하고 1916년 협화대학(協和大學)에 입학하여 1학년을 수료했다. 1920년 귀국하여 1943년까지 중앙고등보통학교에서 영어교사로 봉직했고, 광복 후 고려대학교 교수에 취임했으며, 1949년 대통령 특사로 필리핀에 다녀왔다. 1951년 UN 아시아극동경제위원회 회의에 참석했고, 1955년까지 제3대 외무장관을 역임했으며, 1952년부터 53년까지는 UN에서 한국수석대표로, 1953년에는 국무총리가 되어 외무장관직을 겸했다. 1954년 제네바협상회의에 우리나라 대표로 참석했고, 1956년 이후 서울대 및 고려대 교수로 재직했으며, 1963년 정민회(正民會)를 조직하여 대통령 선거에 출마하기도 했다.

시기로서는 매우 드물면서도 귀한 작업이었다. 실질적으로 첫 사례였던 만큼 완전했다고 할 수는 없지만, 우리의 전통문학을 영문으로 번역하기 위한 모범적 선례를 제시한 점은 변영태의 시조 영역 작업이 지닌 역사적 의미로 기록될 가능성이 크다.

그간 시조의 외국어 번역에 대한 비판적 관점의 의미 있는 연구들이 간간이 출현했다. 시조 일역(日譯)을 제외하고 한역(漢譯)은 상(想) 정도를 옮기는 데 불과했고, 영역 또한 원전에 충실하려 했음에도 독자들에 대한 전달이 완전치 못했음을 지적한 임선묵,[6] 시조의 내적 구조를 의미의 연결이라는 측면에서 간과하지 말아야 하고, 번역된 작품이 시조임을 쉽게 알아 볼 수 있도록 해야 한다는 점 등을 지적한 조태성,[7] 시조다움을 살리는 방향으로 번역이 이루어져야 한다고 강조한 임종찬[8] 등은 현실적 문제점을 바탕으로 시조 번역의 바람직한 길을 꾸준히 제시한 연구들이다. 또한 시조 한역의 사례들을 중심으로 번역의 전통과 지향점을 제시한 연구들,[9] 영역의 실제 사례들을 중심으로 바람직한 방향을 제시한 연구들[10]을 주요 업적으로 꼽을 수 있다.

본고에서는 이런 선행 업적들을 바탕으로 변영태의 영역 시조들이

---

5 특히 *Tales From Korea*와 *Songs From Korea*는 우리문학에 대한 영어 번역의 자매편이라 할 수 있다.

6 「時調의 飜譯問題」, 『東洋學』5, 단국대 동양학연구소, 1975, 22~23쪽 참조.

7 「시조의 외국어 번역에 관한 시론」, 『時調學論叢』31, 한국시조학회, 2009, 218쪽.

8 「현대시조의 진로 모색과 세계화 문제 연구」, 『시조학논총』23, 한국시조학회, 2005, 46쪽.

9 임종찬「시조의 漢詩譯과 漢詩의 時調譯의 문제점 연구」, 『시조학논총』27, 한국시조학회, 2007], 김명순「李滉 時調의 漢譯에 대하여」, 『시조학논총』28, 2008/「시조 한역 자료의 현황과 그 성격」, 『시조학논총』30, 2009], 김주수[漢詩 번역 時調 연구-제 양상과 미발굴 작품을 중심으로-, 『韓國詩歌研究』28, 한국시가학회, 2010] 등의 논의들이 대표적이다.

갖는 모범적 선례로서의 특징과 의미를 찾아보기로 한다.

무슨 의도로 텍스트를 선택하고 번역했나?

변영태는 유명씨 55명[11]과 무명씨들의 작품 총 102편을 골라 번역했다. 대부분 한 작품씩을 들었지만, 이황(6편)·정철(4편)·윤선도(3편)·이명한(3편)·이정신(3편)·조헌(2편)·신흠(2편)·김광욱(2편)·신희문(2편)·안민영(2편) 등 두 편 이상을 든 작자들도 있다. 작자들은 양반 사대부, 중인, 기녀 등인데 기녀를 제외하면 작자들은 대개 현실정치에 참여하던 뛰어난 문인, 학자, 무인, 가객 등이었다. 작자들을 비교적 모든 계층에서 골고루 선정하려 했음을 확인할 수 있다.

---

10 김현숙「時調의 英語飜譯考-英譯에 나타난 表現의 차이를 중심으로」, 『韓國語文學研究』 12, 이화여대 국어국문학회, 1972], 장인식「영역 고시조에 나타난 번역상의 문제점 : 이순신, 이조년, 김종서 시의 경우」, 『번역학연구』 제5권 2호, 2004년 가을], 박진임[앞의 논문] 등은 시조 영역의 여러 측면들을 분석, 제시한 연구들이고, 홍경표「강용흘의 『초당』과 『행복의 숲』에 인용된 한국 〈고시조〉-특히, 영어번역과 관련하여-」, 『한국말글학』 20, 한국말글학회, 2003], 김효중「재미 한인문학에 인용된 고시조 영역 고찰-강용흘의 「초당」을 중심으로」, 『비교문학』 39, 한국비교문학회, 2006] 등은 영어 소설 속에 들어 있는 시조작품들을 대상으로 고시조 영역에 관련되는 문제들을 분석한 결과다.

11 우탁(禹倬)·정몽주(鄭夢周)·정몽주 모친·원천석(元天錫)·변계량(卞季良)·길재(吉再)·성삼문(成三問)·김종서(金宗瑞)·월산대군(月山大君)·송순(宋純)·한호(韓濩)[* 변영태는 한호(韓濩)의 영문표기를 'Han-hwag'이라 했으나, 여기서는 '호'로 해야 맞다.]·이개(李塏)·원호(元昊)·서경덕(徐敬德)·이황(李滉)·김인후(金麟厚)·양사언(楊士彦)·성혼(成渾)·정철(鄭澈)·조헌(趙憲)·이순신(李舜臣)·황진이(黃眞伊)·이원익(李元翼)·이항복(李恒福)·신흠(申欽)·김상헌(金尙憲)·정충신(鄭忠信)·주의식(朱義植)·박인로(朴仁老)·김천택(金天澤)·김진태(金振泰)·김상용(金尙容)·김광욱(金光煜)·윤선도(尹善道)·이명한(李明漢)·조찬한(趙纘韓)·효종(孝宗)·정태화(鄭太和)·강백년(姜栢年)·송시열(宋時烈)·남구만(南九萬)·박태보(朴泰輔)·김창업(金昌業)·김영(金煐)·이정보(李鼎輔)·김수장(金壽長)·김우규(金友奎)·송종원(宋宗元)·이정신(李廷藎)·신희문(申喜文)·명옥(明玉)·박효관(朴孝寬)·이중집(李仲集)·안민영(安玟英) 등이 그들이다.

수록작품에 대하여 번역자는 다음과 같은 입장을 밝혔다.

이 책의 노래들은 작가가 밝혀진 작품들의 경우는 생년월일의 순으로, 출생 연도가 확실치 않은 경우엔 그 작가가 살았다고 알려진 시대의 왕계(王系)의 순서에 따랐다. 무명씨의 시작품들은 별다른 수록방침 없이 필자와 출판사가 임의로 선택한 순서대로 수록했다. 모든 옛 노래들은 제목이 없는데, 실제로 시조의 간결함이 그에 대한 충분한 해명이 될 듯도 하다. 어떤 의미에서 그들은 수록작품들 스스로가 제목이기 때문이다. 그러나 이 작품들은 서로가 마치 교도소 내의 많은 수인(囚人)들과 비슷하게 각자 편리하게 번호로 매겨졌다. 작가들의 약력은 노래들을 스스로 낭송하고 읽는데 방해가 되지 않도록 배려하여 책의 말미에 알파벳 순으로 수록하였다. 그것으로 흥미가 더해지고 노래들 자체의 이해에 크게 일조할 것을 희망한다.[12]

---

12 Y.T.Pyun, Foreword, Songs from Korea, Cheongjin Seo-gwan, 1936. : Those songs whose authors are known are arranged either in the order of their birth dates or, where they can not be ascertained, according to the order of the kings whom they are known to have served. Then follow the anonymous poems in no sort of arrangement at all. They just jostle along as we do. All of the old songs have no themes. Indeed, their being so short might constitute an adequate excuse for having none at all. In a sense, they are themes themselves. However, they look like one another as so many prison inmates so that they are as conveniently numbered.
To allow the songs to speak for themselves and let nothing interrupt their reading, the biographical notes are attached at the end of the book in the alphabetical order. But interest is hoped to be added thereby and much light thrown on the interpretation of the songs themselves.[*본 인용문의 원문은 민충환 교수(부천대 명예교수)가 타자(打字)하여 엮은 원고본에서 따온 것이고, 이하 '머리말' 인용문들은 김영배 선생의 번역을 가져오되 필자가 약간씩의 수정을 가한 것이다. *Songs from Korea*의 사진자료를 제공해주신 민 교수께 감사드린다.]

인용문에서 눈에 띄는 것은 번역자가 옛 시조들을 '노래'와 '시작품'이란 두 개념으로 받아들이고 있다는 점이다. 또한 각각의 작품들에 제목을 달지 않은 점도 '시조의 간결함'에서 그 이유를 찾고 있다. 또한 '수록된 노래들 하나하나가 제목 그 자체'라고 했는데, 이 점은 옛 시조의 즉흥성을 지적한 말이다. 특별히 제목을 전제로 하지 않고 물건이나 사실에 직면하여 감정을 불러일으키는 것이 옛 시조의 본질임을 강조한 것이다. 작자들의 약력을 작품에 덧붙이지 않고 뒤에 수록한 것은 그것들이 작품 이해에 선입견으로 작용하는 것을 막고자 했기 때문이라고 했다. 또한 번역자는 대상 작품들을 비교적 골고루 선정하겠다는 의도를 피력했다. 그것은 102편의 작품에 유명씨 작가 55명과 상당수의 무명씨 작가들을 배당한 점으로도 알 수 있다. 번역자는 자신이 선정한 옛 시조 작품들과 작가들이야말로 우리의 옛 시조장르를 대표한다는 자부심을 갖고 있었으며, 우리의 옛 시조를 전 세계의 잠재적 독자 특히 영어권 독자들에게 보여주고자 하는 의지를 강하게 드러냈다고 할 수 있다.

작품들의 주제 역시 탄노(歎老)·충절(忠節)·교훈(敎訓)·회고(懷古)·신념(信念)·우국(憂國)·자적(自適)·안빈(安貧)·번민(煩悶)·연모(戀慕)·자연친화(自然親和)·허무(虛無)·취락(醉樂)[혹은 향락(享樂)]·풍자(諷刺)·효친(孝親)·한거(閑居)·망향(望鄕)·홍(興)·자탄(自歎)·원망(怨望) 등으로 다양한데, 여기서 옛 시조가 본질적으로 낭만시의 범주에 속하긴 하나 주제적 측면에서는 현실과 낭만이 적절한 조화를 이루고 있다는 점을 확인하게 되며, 현실과 꿈을 바탕으로 삶의 전반적인 면을 보여주고자 한 번역자의 의도 또한 분명히 드러난다고 할 수 있다. 실제 몇 작품을 들어 이런 그의 의도를 살펴보기로 한다.

The ancients saw me not, nor do

I them. Though they are out of sight,

The path they walked still runs aglow

In front o' me. Since the path of light

The ancients fared on lies before,

Why should I waver any more?

〈I-hwang〉

이 번역작품을 우리말로 다시 번역하면 다음과 같다.

선조들도 나를 보지 못했고,

나 또한 그들을 보지 못했네.

그들은 보이지 않지만,

그들이 걸었던 길은 여전히 내 앞에서 빛을 내네.

옛날 선조들이 걸었던 길이 있으니

내가 어찌 흔들리겠는가?

〈拙譯〉

이 작품의 원작은 이황의 〈도산육곡(陶山六曲)〉 가운데 두 번째 그룹[언학(言學)]의 세 번째 노래[13]를 번역한 것이다. 원작자가 작품을 통해 말하고자 한 바를 정확히 옮긴 경우가 바로 이것이다. '배움의

---

13 심재완, 『校本 歷代時調全書』, 세종문화사, 1972, 69쪽, No.187[古人도 날 몯보고 나도 古人 몯뵈古人를 못봐도 녀던 길 알픠 잇닉녀던 길 알픠 잇거든 아니 녀고 엇뎔고] 참조. 이하 이 책의 이름과 가번(歌番)을 통해 번역 대상으로 삼은 고시조 작품의 출처를 밝힌다.

길'을 제시하고자 했는데, 매우 현실적인 문제를 노래로 승화시킨 셈이다. 이처럼 번역자가 원작자의 생각에 공감할 경우 원작의 의도나 내용을 비교적 정확히 축어적(逐語的)으로 옮기고자 마음먹은 듯하다. 다만 '알픠 잇닉'를 '내 앞에서 빛을 내네'로 '아니 녀고 엇덜고'를 '내가 어찌 흔들리겠는가?'로 바꾼 경우들이 눈에 띄는데, 오히려 원작자의 생각에 미적 수사를 가미함으로써 그 의미를 강조한 결과라고 할 수 있다. 단순히 '앞에 있다'고 하는 대신 '빛을 낸다'고 한 것이나, '아니 가고 어쩌리?'라 하지 않고 '어찌 흔들리겠는가?'라고 함으로써 훌륭한 선조들이 닦아놓은 삶의 지혜를 배우겠다는 의지를 효과적으로 부각시키는 데 성공했다고 본다. 번역자가 이황의 이 작품을 선택하여 비교적 충실하게 옮겼고, 핵심적인 부분에서 좀 더 세련된 표현으로 바꾼 것은 그 자신이 이 작품에 표현된 원작자의 인생관이나 세계관에 공감하는바 컸기 때문일 것이다. 번역자 자신도 배움에 대한 신념을 강하게 지니고 있었다는 점은 이황의 이 작품을 축어역(逐語譯)에 가까울 정도로 정확히 옮겨놓은 점에서 확인된다.

그러나 연모를 주제로 하는 작품의 경우는 좀 더 번역자의 창안이 많이 반영된 것으로 보인다. 말하자면 자신의 생각과 부합하는 현실적인 문제나 특정 이념 혹은 신념의 시조를 번역할 경우 정확하게 옮겨놓음으로써 원작의 뜻을 손상시키지 않고자 했으나, 그와 달리 연모(戀慕)와 같은 서정의 세계에서는 스스로 자유롭고자 한 모습을 발견하게 된다. 다음과 같은 경우다.

Would that my heart into the moon

Could be transformed, exalted hung

In the blue with no cloudy dune

And represent this speechless tongue,

Flooding with light where my lord lies

Unconscious of my grief and sighs.

〈Jung-chul〉

이 작품은 다음과 같이 직역된다.

나의 마음, 달로 바꾸어

구름 없는 파란 하늘에 올리고

이 말없는 혀를 대신하고 빛으로 흘러서

님 계신 그곳을,

나의 탄식과 한숨을 모르게 하여

비추어 보리.

〈졸역〉

인용한 영문시는 정철의 원작[14]을 번역한 작품이다. 정철의 원작에 나오는 '님'은 대부분 임금으로 치환된다고 보는 것이 일반적이다. 그만큼 관인으로 살아가면서 생사를 넘나드는 부침(浮沈)을 경험한 그였기에 권력의 정점인 임금을 '님'으로 치환하여 자신의 간절한 감정을 투사하는 일이야말로 생존 본능에 가까운 정치적 수사의 필연적 이유였을 것이다. 그러나 이 노래에서 1차적으로 표면화 되는 정서는 이성 간의 연모다. 정철이 본질적으로 추구한 것은 이성에 대한 연모의 정이었으나, 작자 스스로 현실적 맥락에서는 연군(戀君)으로 읽혀

---

14 심재완, 『교본 역대시조전서』, 198쪽 No.566[내 ᄆᆞ음 버혀 내여 별들을 밍글고져구 만리 댱텬의 번드시 걸려이셔고은 님 계신 고ᄃᆡ 가 비최여나 보리라] 참조.

지기를 바랐을 것이다. 이 점이 정철을 비롯한 사대부 문학의 이중성이다. '님'을 번역하는 일이 어렵다는 점을 변영태는 다음과 같이 설명했다.

> 시조작품의 해석에서 '님'이라는 단어가 종종 등장하는데, 많은 것들이 이 단어의 의미를 여하히 해석하는가에 달려 있다. 이 독특한 단어의 존재는 반드시 시조를 일견(一見) 사랑의 단가(短歌)처럼 보이도록 하는데, 가끔은 그렇지 않은 경우도 있다. 그 단어는 종종 "내가 헌신(獻身)하는 사람" 좀 더 정확히는 "나를 소유하고 있는 사람"을 의미한다. 많은 경우들에서 이 단어는 왕 또는 다른 헌신의 대상을 상징하기도 한다. 작품들의 번역에서 이 단어의 혼돈을 없애려는 시도를 해왔다.[15]

변영태 역시 '님'을 연모의 대상이자 충성의 대상으로 파악하고 있었음을 알 수 있다. 사실 정서적으로나 본능적으로는 이성 간의 연모를 그려내고자 하면서도 사회적 제재(制裁)의 위험성을 피해갈 수 있는 장치나 방도를 마련해 두고자 했던 것이 전통시대의 문인들이었다. 그 '님'을 변영태는 'lord'라 했다. 'lord'는 영어권에서 '사람들에 대하여 힘과 통제력 혹은 권위를 지닌 인물'을 지칭하는 말이다.[16] 그

---

15 Y.T.Pyun, Foreword, Songs from Korea : In the interpretation of a "si-jo", much depends upon how you make out the meaning of the term "nim" which frequently occurs. The presence of this peculiar word necessarily makes the poem look like a love ditty. But it is as often not as it is. The word means "the one to whom I am devoted", or more exactly, "the one who possesses me." In many cases, it signifies the king or any other object of devotion. In the translations, an attempt has been made to remove the confusion.

16 Random House Webster'sCollege Dictionary, New York : Random House, 1997, p.777.

러니 '사랑하는 이성의 대상'과 '왕조시대의 임금'을 동시에 포괄하는 '님'을 그런 말로나 바꾸어 놓을 수밖에 없었을 것이다. 번역자가 파악한 '님'이 단순히 사랑하는 대상이었다면, 차라리 'honey'로 바꾸는 편이 무난했을 것이다. 그러나 번역자는 정철 노래의 '님'이 이중적 의미를 지닌 용어임을 알고 있었기 때문에, 'lord'라 번역하고 그 말 이외의 다른 부분에서는 사랑하는 이성 간에 오갈 수 있는 감정적 교류를 암시해 놓았던 것이다. 말하자면 'lord'는 결코 사랑하는 이성을 지칭하는 말은 될 수 없기 때문에 감정을 그려내는 표현들을 통해 이성 간에 오갈 수 있는 사랑의 감정을 드러낸 것이다. 말하자면 그는 이 부분에서 애매성을 통한 의미의 이중성을 무리 없이 옮기는 데 성공했다고 할 수 있다.

　이처럼 번역자는 원작자 정철의 실제 삶이나 현실적 성향을 떠올렸을 것이고, 환로(宦路)에서 겪은 수난들과 함께 그가 남긴 많은 시조들의 의미적 이중성을 생각하면서 '님'이란 소재가 갖는 복합적 의미를 무리 없이 담을 수 있는 말을 찾아내고자 노력했을 것이다.[17] 꽤 거리가 있는 두 의미를 하나의 단어에 포괄해온 정철의 노래들에 흥미를 느꼈고, 그런 모호한 말을 번역하여 서구인들에게 보여줌으로써 의식의 보편성을 스스로 확인하고자 한 점에 그의 의도가 들어 있었다고 볼만하다.

---

17 조규익, 『풀어읽는 우리 노래문학』, 논형, 2007, 214쪽.

번역에 대한 변영태의 관점

도남(陶南) 조윤제(趙潤濟)는 '자국문학을 외국어로 역출(譯出)하는 것은 세계의 평가를 받자는 것인데, 고래(古來) 조선학자의 조선시가 한역(漢譯)은 그 의미가 어디 있었는가가 심히 의문이며 조선어 자체에 대한 멸시 즉 바꾸어 말하면 한문에 대한 무조건의 숭상으로부터 나온 기현상'[18]이라고 비판한 적이 있다. 과거에 성행했던 우리 노래의 한역 자세나 풍토에 대한 비판이지만, 역으로 이 글을 쓴 시기와 변영태가 시조를 영역했던 시기가 크게 멀지 않았기 때문에 당시의 학자나 문인들은 우리 시가의 외국어역에 관한 관심이나 필요성을 얼마간 공감하고 있었음에 틀림없다.

비슷한 시기 안서(岸曙) 김억(金億)은 시가 번역의 어려움을 토로한 바 있다. 완역(完譯)이란 불가능하니 '원작의 뜻이나 따다가 역자가 자기 식으로 다시 창작할 수밖에 없다'[19]는 것이다. 안서는 서구시를 우리말로 번역하거나 한시를 우리말로 번역함으로써 신문학 초기 우리 문단에서 번역문학의 선구적 위치에 서 있던 인물이다. 도남은 우리 시가를 외국어로 번역하는 사람들의 태도나 정신을 비판했고, 안서는 외국 시가를 우리말로 번역하는 어려움을 강조했는데, 얼핏 양자의 관점이 서로 다른 것처럼 보이지만 본질은 그렇지 않다. 도남이 비판한 현상의 내면에 우리 시가를 외국어로 번역하는 일이나 외국 시를 우리말로 번역하는 일이 수월치 않다는 현실인식이 도사리고 있으니, 궁극적으로 도남과 안서의 생각은 일치한다고 할 수 있다. 이들이 이러한 고민을 안고 있던 것과 비슷한 시기에 시조를 영역한

---

18 조윤제, 「詩歌漢譯과 龍飛御天歌(一)」, 동아일보 1936. 1. 19.
19 홍순석 편, 『岸曙金億全集 ③ 漢詩譯集』, 한국문화사, 1987, 725쪽.

변영태 또한 같은 고민을 안고 있었으리라 본다. 변영태는 시조 번역의 어려움을 다음과 같이 설명했다.

　　이들 한국의 노래들은 대개 짧은 시들로 되어 있다.-그 아름다움의 많은 부분은 제재(題材)에 있지 않고 소리로 간결하게 표현되는 말들의 음악성에 있는데, 그것은 그 아름다움이 말하는 사물이나 내용에 있다는 것이 아니라 그들이 입으로 어떻게 읽는가에 있음을 의미한다. 번역을 하는 데 있어 전자의 경우는 다른 언어로의 변환작업이 비교적 쉽게 이루어지는 반면 후자의 경우는 그리 녹록치 않다. 만약 당신이 음악이나 마술(魔術)을 다른 언어로 번역하는 데 성공한다면 그것은 행운이며 감사해야 할 일이지 널리 자랑할 거리는 못되며 마찬가지로 당신이 실패했더라도 그것은 흔히 일어날 일이 일어난 것일 뿐 그리 나쁜 것은 아니다. 이 점은 바로 시조를 번역하기가 힘들다는 것임을 의미한다. 엄밀히 말해서 그렇다. 하지만 불가능이란 항상 목표로 설정하여 투쟁하는 대상일진대, 시조라고 거기서 예외가 될 순 없지 않은가? 이 좋은 머리를 그저 방치할 것인가? 아니다, 그건 아니다. 인간으로서 가진 이 특권을 포기해선 안 된다. 우리는 시의 이해에 대한 노력을 꾸준히 하여야 하며 뜻이 교묘하여 이해하기 어려운 작품이어서 비록 그 일부를 포기할지언정 가능한 모든 상상의 나래를 펼쳐 시의 세계라는 축복의 땅으로 진입하는 노력을 꾸준히 하여야 한다.[20]

　변영태가 옛 시조의 본질을 꿰뚫고 있던 인물이었음은 이 글에서도 확인된다. 시조가 지닌 아름다움의 큰 부분은 노래된 소재나 주제 등 내용에서 찾기 보다는 낭독할 때 중시되는 성조(聲調)에서 찾아야 한다는 것을 강조한 내용으로도 그 점은 분명해진다. 한 작품

의 내용은 번역하기 쉽지만, 성조는 번역하기 어렵다는 것이 그의 주
장이다. 그것은 음악이나 미술을 다른 언어로 번역하기 어려운 것과
같은 일이라고 했다. 그래서 그런 것들을 다른 언어로 번역하는 데
성공했다면 감사할 일이지만, 실패했다고 해서 비난 받을 일도 아니
라는 것이다.

시조 영역의 큰 부분은 성조에 관한 것이므로 번역에 성공한다면
좋은 일이지만, 실패했다 하여 절망하거나 비난 받을 일은 아니라는
점을 강조하기 위해 그런 사례를 들었다고 볼 수 있다. 말하자면 자
신의 번역에 대하여 나올 수 있는 비판의 예봉을 미리 꺾어두기 위한
전략이었을 것이다. 그러나 그에 그치지 않고, 열심히 노력하여 시조
를 영어로 번역하는 데 성공함으로써 본격적인 '시의 세계'로 진입할
수 있도록 해야 한다는 것이 변영태 주장의 진실이다. 말하자면 자신
의 시조 영역이 성공했든 실패했든 그것은 본질적인 번역의 어려움
때문이지 번역자의 능력 때문은 아니라는 점을 강조함으로써 자신의

---

20 Y.T.Pyun, Foreword, Songs from Korea : It is with most of these Korean songs as
with short poems in general — much of the beauty lies in their music of words
reducible to sound, not in the subject matter, that is, not so much in the things
they say as in how they read orally. The former can be easily transplanted in
another language, but, as to the latter, nothing definite can be said. If you succeed
in conveying the music, the magic, too, then you are fortunate, a thing to be
thankful for, not to be proud of. If you fail, you have done what was reasonably
expected to be done, no worse. This amounts to admitting that poetry is not
amenable to translation. Strictly speaking, yes. But impossibilities are always
aimed at, strived for. And why not this particular one? What is the use of our
being furnished with a better brain after all? No, no, it would not do to waive this
human prerogative. We must go on torturing poems, and. when what is elusive
eludes, leaving something imbecile, we are not to despair but to make the best of
the situation by imagining ourselves into the bliss that would be ours if what has
apparently eluded had not.

번역 결과에 대한 불안감을 해소하려 한 동시에 좋은 번역을 지향하여 끊임없이 노력해야 한다는 의지 또한 표명한 셈이다.

그렇다면 그는 시조의 본질을 어떻게 파악하고 있었을까. 다음의 인용문에 분명히 드러난다.

시조는 중국의 시와는 구별되는 오랜 전통을 가진 순수 한국어로 된 시가 형식이다. 시조는 영국의 소네트와 거의 유사한 규칙성을 가지고 있는데, 차이점이라면 시가의 구절이 소네트의 반 정도라는 것뿐이다. 또한 그 짧은 형식에도 불구하고 고유의 구절들도 가지고 있다. 시조는 본질적으로 노래 부르기 위한 장르이며 가끔 기쁠 때 즉흥적으로 노래되기도 한다. 시조의 연원(淵源)에 대한 정확한 기록은 없지만, 이 유일한 고유의 시가형태는 800여 년 동안 꾸준히 이어져 왔다. 약간의 추측성 속단을 해본다면, 그 기원은 좀 더 이른 시대로 거슬러 올라갈 수도 있다. 거의 모든 단시(短詩) 종류들이 그렇듯이 시조도 그 형태에 있어서 간단명료하며 또한 지루하게 한 문장으로 길게 늘어지지 않고 적절한 구절로 단락 지어진다.

옳건 그르건, 시조 작가들은 윌리엄 워즈워드처럼 작시(作詩)를 심오한 업으로 삼는 사람들이 거의 없으며 시조라는 형식으로 흉중(胸中)을 털어놓는다는 점에서 더더욱 그러하다. 시조작가들이 좌우간 시를 썼다면, 그들은 무언가 할 말이 있기 때문만이 아니라 그것을 가볍고 즐겁게 말하려 했기 때문에 쓴 것이다. 이 점이 바로 시조의 행들에서 어떤 강렬한 설교나 깊은 철학이 발견되지 않는다는 점을 분명히 보여준다. 그 이유는 시조작가들이 확고한 사상을 가지고 있지 못해서가 아니라 그들이 적어도 시조에서만큼은 심오한 사상을 심기 싫어서였을 것이다. 독자들은 이 책에 실려 있는 어떤 시조들은 작자들의 실제 모습과는 다소 다르다는 점을 발견하게 될 것이다. 그것은 작가들이 한가하고 자의식이 강하지 않은 상태에서 작품을 썼는데, 그런 경우의 작품들은 그들이 말한 모든 것을 나타내지는 않는다. …많은 시조들에는 자연 사랑이 스며들어 있는데, 그것은 신앙적인 숭배의 모습이라기보다는 건전한 자연예찬 종류들이며 그 표현방식도 복잡다단하거나 과장된 형식이 아닌 평이하며 사랑 어린 것들이 대부분이다. 이러한 자연예찬의 형식은 새로이 시작된 것이며 필요에 따라 편안함을 주는 역할도 한다.[21]

---

21 Y.T.Pyun, Foreword, Songs from Korea : "Si-jo" is the time-honoured form of poetry in pure Korean tongue, distinct from those of Chinese poems. It has almost all the regularity of the English sonnet, only shorter by half. It has its own pauses, too, in spite of its shortness. It is essentially a thing to be sung, and has often been improvised on occasions of rejoicings. There is no dating it back exactly, but it would be quite safe to say that this sole form of vernacular versification has been in constant use for these 800 years. If one swallow is allowed to make the summer, its history extends further back. As all such simple things should, it must be lucid, direct, single in point, and yet it must not be one trailing sentence with no pause, plausibly chopped into lines.

Rightly or wrongly, none of our poets has ever made a serious business of poetry to the degree that Wordsworth did, far less in expressing themselves with "si-jo". If they wrote poetry at all, they did so not merely because they had something to say, but also because they could say it lightly and playfully. This throws light on the fact that neither fierce preaching nor deep philosophy is to be found in their lines of verse. It is not that they were incapable of sustained thought but that they would have sooner put down serious ideas in anything else but poetry. You will find that some of the songs here given are somewhat out of keeping with the general delineations of their authors' characters. That simply means that they were off guard, not self-conscious, and then that often they did not mean all they said.···Many of the songs are pervaded with a love of Nature, perhaps of a most sane sort, never so deep as to be akin to worship, neither morbid in any manner, but just enough to render life tolerable — in a word, a chummy sort of love, never tired, never surfeited. It is quite a something to start with and, if need be, to fall back upon.

시조가 중국 시와 구별되는 반면 영국의 소네트와는 유사한 규칙성을 갖고 있었다고 하는데, 중국 시와 영국시를 함께 들어 대비시킨 것은 자신이 시도하는 시조 영역의 당위성을 강조하려는 의도였을 것이다. 시조가 '중국 시와 구별되는 오랜 전통을 가진 순수 한국어로 된 시가'임을 강조함으로써 근대 이전에 성행했던 시조의 한역이 시조의 본질 상 그다지 탐탁한 일은 아니었음과 시조의 영역이 시대정신에 맞는 일임을 암시했다고 할 수 있다.

무엇보다도 그가 시조를 '본질적으로 노래 부르기 위한 장르'로 본 점은 당시의 인식수준으로 볼 때 탁월한 견해다. 근대 이전이라면 시조가 노래 부르기 위한 장르라는 인식쯤은 별스럽지 않았을 것이나, 시조부흥론 시기부터 변영태의 활동시기에 걸치는 시기의 지식인으로서 '시조가 노래'라는 인식을 갖는 것은 결코 쉬운 일이 아니었다. 시조부흥운동을 거치면서 우리의 문단이나 학계에 고착된 오해들 가운데 하나는 '시조가 우리 고유의 시'라는 편견이었다. 시조가 '노래이면서 시'라는 인식을 가질 수 없을 만큼 당대 시조 부흥론자들의 생각은 지나치게 완고했다. 당시 시조부흥운동을 주도했던 인사들이 우리말로 시를 짓던 시인들이었기 때문에 전통 시조를 시형의 하나로만 인식하려고 했던 것이다.[22]

이와 달리 변영태는 시조가 노래라는 인식을 갖고 있었으며, '기쁠 때 즉흥적으로 노래되기도 한다'고 했다. 시조가 노래라는 인식을 갖고 있었기 때문에 시조의 내용이 심오하지 않다는 점에 대하여 크게 개의하지 않을 수 있었던 것이다. 그가 말한 것처럼 시조 작가들은 서양의 윌리엄 워즈워드처럼 작시를 심오한 업으로 생각하지 않았으

---

22 조규익, 「안자산의 시조론에 대하여」, 『時調學論叢』 30, 한국시조학회, 2009, 185쪽.

며, 가볍게 흥중을 털어 놓거나 수시로 일어나는 감흥을 즐겁게 말하려 했기 때문에 시조에서 '강렬한 설교나 깊은 철학이 발견되지 않는다'고 했다. 그러나 시조작자들의 사상이 천박해서가 아니라 시조에서만큼은 심오한 사상을 언술(言述)하고 싶지 않아서였기 때문이라 했다. 말하자면 시조를 하나의 유흥적 표현수단으로 생각했을 뿐 사상과 철학을 담은 담론체계로 인식하지는 않았다는 것이다. 그래서 그는 시조가 '신앙적 숭배의 모습'을 띠지 않은, '건전한 자연예찬의 종류들'로서 '과장되지 않고 평이한 형식'의 노래장르일 수 있다는 견해를 갖고 있었다.

변영태가 영어 번역에의 의욕을 가질 수 있었던 것도 그가 시조의 본질을 제대로 인식하고 있었기 때문이다. 특히 언어적 짜임의 규칙성이나 시정신이 한시보다는 영시와 통한다고 본 점은 시조의 영역에 선뜻 나서게 된 동기로 작용했으리라 추측된다.

미국에 정착한 강용흘이 자신의 소설에서 시조를 영어로 번역하여 인용한 것[23]을 시조 영역의 첫 사례로 꼽을 수는 있지만, 뚜렷한 목적과 방향 위에서 행한 시조 영역으로는 변영태가 실질적인 첫 사례라 할 수 있다. 선례 없는 작업에 망설임 없이 나설 수 있었던 것도 시조와 영시 양자의 본질 모두를 꿰뚫고 있었던 그의 소양 덕분이었을 것이다.[24]

그렇다면 우리말로 이루어진 원작과 현격하게 다른 번역시의 운율은 어떻게 처리했을까? 무엇보다 두드러진 점은 모든 번역시에서 각운(脚韻)을 정확하게 처리했다는 점이다. 예컨대 황진이의 〈청산리

---

23 강용흘의 『초당(The Grass Roof)』과 『행복한 숲(The Happy Grove)』에는 모두 31편의 번역시조가 인용되어 있다.[홍경표, 「강용흘의 『초당』과 『행복의 숲』에 인용된 한국 〈고시조〉」, 『한국말글학』 20, 한국말글학회, 2003, 318~319쪽.]

벽계수야~〉를 그는 다음과 같이 번역했다.[25]

> You boisterous torrent, why so haste,
>
> So dashing over rocky bed,
>
> And boast your speed and pride thus taste?
>
> All's over when to th' sea you 've sped
>
> To turn no more. Then why not stay,
>
> Linger by moonlit hills and play?
>
> 〈Hwang-jin-i〉

'haste-bed-taste-sped-stay-play'의 배치에서 보듯이 번역시의 각운은 정확하고 명쾌한 'ababcc형(型)'으로 이루어져 있다. 내용과 연관 지어 보았을 때도 매우 정교하다. 앞부분 네 행은 물의 흐름 곧 움직임을 다루고 있으므로 'abab'의 반복과 변화를 추구했고, 뒷부분 두 행은 '쉬어 감'의 소망(所望)을 드러낸 까닭에 각운의 변화를 주지 않고 'cc형'으로 고정시킨 것이다. 각운 못지않게 시 내부의 운율도 '약강 4보격[iambic tetrameter]'으로 절묘하게 짜여져 있다.[26] 위 번역

---

24 번역이란 단순히 한 언어에서 다른 언어로 치환하는 작업만은 아니다. 번역자는 양쪽의 문화에 상당한 정도의 통찰력을 갖고 있어야 한다. 이 점에 대하여 김지원은 "복잡한 번역현장에서 가장 필요한 것은 번역자가 두 언어의 常用능력 뿐 아니라 양국 문화에 대해 통찰력 있는 비전을 갖는 것이다. 번역자들은 의미의 전환 과정에 나타나는 부조화들을 극복하려고 시도하면서 이데올로기와 도덕체계, 사회-정치 구조 등을 포함하는 문화들 사이에서 창조적인 중재 역할을 수행한다"[「번역학의 어제와 오늘」, 『번역학연구』 제5권 1호, 한국번역학회, 2004년 봄, 69~70쪽]고 주장했는데, 궁극적으로 번역자는 '새로운 문화의 창조자'가 되어야 한다는 말이다.

25 황진이의 작품을 예로 들어 운율을 분석한 것은 그의 작품이 고금을 통하여 많이 애창되어 익숙하다고 보았기 때문이다. 여타 작품들의 운율구조도 이와 거의 같은 양상을 보여준다.

시의 운율을 분석하면 다음과 같다.

You **boist** | erous **torr** | ent, ‖ **why** | so **haste**,
약 강　약약 강　약　강　약　강

So **da** | shing **ov** | er **rock** | y **bed**,
약 강　약 강　약 강　약 강

And **boast** | your **speed** | and **pride** | thus **taste**?
약　강　약　강　약　강　약　강

All's **ov** | er **when** | to th' se | you 've **sped**
약 강약 강　약 강　약　강

To **turn** | no **more**. ‖ Then **why** | not **stay**,
약 강　약 강　약 강　약 강

Linger | by **moonl** | it **hills** | and **play**?
강 약　약 강　약 강　약　강

　밑줄 그은 두 부분[약 약 강/강 약]에 약간의 예외가 있기는 하지만, 이것은 의도적으로 설정한 변화라고 보아야 할 것이다. 특히, 마지막 행 첫 낱말 linger의 '강약'격은 화자가 벽계수의 행동을 촉구하고 있다는 점을 고려하면 첫 음절에 '강'을 배치한 것이 오히려 자연스럽다고 할 수 있다. 번역자는 또한 중세 영시의 유산(遺産)인 행중(行中)

---

26 변영태도 서문에서 예로 들었듯이 영시의 대표적 정형시인 소네트의 경우 '약강 5보격[iambic pentameter]'이지만 시조의 4음보를 염두에 두고 있었으므로 그는 4보격으로 번역한 것 같다.

휴지(休止)[caesura : ‖]를 첫 행과 다섯째 행에서 쓰고 있는데, 이 점은 시적 화자가 전하고자 하는 중요 메시지의 변화를 암시하는 효과도 발휘한다고 볼 수 있다. 그런데, 넷째 행에서 'when' 대신 'once'로 썼어야 '일도창해하면'의 불회귀성(不回歸性)을 적극적으로 표현할 수 있었으리라 보지만, 번역자가 굳이 'when'을 사용한 것은 다음 행의 'Then'과의 음성적 조화를 의식했던 까닭이라고 생각된다.[27] 이런 점에서 본다면 변영태의 시조 영역은 내용적인 면 뿐 아니라 운율 등 형식적인 면에서도 탁월한 모습을 보여준다고 할 수 있다.

번역자의 번역방식과 의미

그는 동아일보[1935년 10월~1936년 1월]에 모두 61수의 옛 시조들과 그에 대한 영역작품들을 연재했고, 나중에 자신이 창작한 32작품의 영시들과 함께 그것들을 SONGS FROM KOREA에 실었다. 그는 모든 시조들을 여섯 개의 라인(line)으로 번역했는데, 아마도 시조의 '6구'를 염두에 둔 결과일 것이다. 대부분의 번역시들은 원작자의 의도를 충실히 재현한 경우와 번역자의 해석적 견해를 가미한 경우 등 두 가지 성향들을 보여준다. 어떤 것이 바람직한 번역인지는 관점에 따라 다를 것이다. 그의 번역 작품들을 앞에 제시한 두 범주로 나누어 살펴보고자 한다.

---

27 이상 변영태 영역 시조의 운율분석[scansion]에 결정적인 도움을 준 백정국 교수[숭실대 영문과]께 감사드린다.

첫째, 원작자 의도를 충실히 재현한 경우

변영태의 영역시조들 가운데 가장 큰 비중을 차지하는 것이 원작자의 의도를 충실하게 재현하려고 한 경우다. 그는 풍자와 은유 등 시조의 수사적 표현과 미적 바탕을 분명히 알고 있었기 때문에 원작자의 의도를 충실히 재현할 수 있었다. 존 드라이든(John Dryden)은 번역의 세 유형들[직역(metaphrase)/의역(paraphrase)/모방(imitation)]을 제시한 다음 가장 바람직한 유형을 직역과 모방의 중간 즉 의역이라고 했는데,[28] 그 말은 원작자의 정신적·문화적 배경을 숙지해야 하고, 두 언어에 능통해야 함을 의미한다. 그럴 경우 원작자의 의도를 재현한다는 것은 직역보다는 의역에 가까운 번역행위라고 보아야 할 것이다. 몇 작품들을 살펴보기로 한다.

> Life is, at most, a hundred years;
>
> Wealth and fame, aren't they but a cloud!
>
> Leaving the world, its joys and fears,
>
> A cot far from the busy crowd
>
> I made my home; hills seemed to say,
>
> "O why did you so long delay?"
>
> ⟨Sin- heui-moon⟩

---

28 John Dryden, Preface to Ovid's Epistles, Translation/History/Culture ; A Source Book, Ed. André Lefevere, London and New York ; Routledge, 1992, pp.102~105.

이 작품의 원작29은 신희문(申喜文)이 지은 것으로『육당본 청구영언』에 285번째로 실려 있다. 그는 15수 정도의 시조를 남긴 인물로 정조 때 생존했던 것으로 추정된다. 남긴 작품들을 살펴보면, 그는 전원에 숨어 안빈낙도하며 인생을 관조하던 지식인이었던 듯하다. 번역시에서는 '탈세속 귀전원(脫世俗 歸田園)'의 모티프를 담담하면서도 결기(決氣) 있게 표출하고 있는데, 세상의 부귀공명을 헛되이 여겨 세상일을 던져 버리고 산당(山堂)으로 들어간 감회를 담담하게 노래한 것이 원작의 내용이다. 우선 번역시를 우리말로 번역해 보면 다음과 같다.

> 인생은 길어야 백년이라네 ;
> 부와 명예 모두 뜬구름에 지나지 않는다네!
> 세상을 등지며, 그 기쁨과 두려움,
> 바쁜 사람들로부터 멀어져
> 나는 집에 돌아왔네 ; 산은 나에게
> "왜 이리 늦게 왔느냐?"고 묻는 듯하네
>
> 〈졸역〉

번역시는 원작을 거의 그대로 재현해 놓은 수준임을 확인할 수 있다. "인생천지백년간(人生天地百年間)에"→"인생은 길어야 백년이라네", "부귀공명여부운(富貴功名如浮雲)을"→"부와 명예 모두 뜬구름에 지나지 않는다네!", "세사(世事)를 후리치고"→"세상을 등지며, 그 기쁨과 두려움, 바쁜 사람들로부터 멀어져", "청산(靑山)이 날다려 이

---

29 심재완,『교본 역대시조전서』, 859쪽 No.2407[人生天地 百年間에 富貴功名 如浮雲을 世事를 후리치고 山堂으로 돌아오니 靑山이 날다려 니르기를 더듸 왓다 ᄒ더라] 참조.

르기를 더듸 왓다 ᄒ더라"→"산은 나에게 '왜 이리 늦게 왔느냐?'고 묻는 듯하네." 등으로 원작과 번역시의 구절 각각은 같은 의미와 비중으로 대응된다. 세사(世事)를 '세상, 기쁨과 두려움, 바쁜 사람들'로 풀어 놓았을 뿐 전체 시상은 축어역(逐語譯)에 가까운 '1:1 대응'이다. 원작의 주제나 시상이 뚜렷하여 중의적(重義的) 해석의 가능성이 없을 뿐 아니라, 시적 형상화 자체가 뛰어날 경우, 원작의 내용이나 의도를 가감 없이 번역시에 재현하고자 한 번역자의 입장이 분명히 드러난다. 또 한 작품을 들기로 한다.

> Let us be changed in after life,
>
> You become I and then I you,
>
> You pine for me in wasting strife
>
> As I have done all my life through,
>
> And maybe you'll experience
>
> What pain I've borne-my sole defence!
>
> ⟨Anon.⟩

이 작품은 작자를 알 수 없는 시조를 번역한 경우다. 남녀 중의 하나가 애정에 성실치 못한 상대[혹은 시큰둥한 상대]에게 늘어놓은 하소연 혹은 푸념을 절묘하게 표현한 노래로서 『청구영언』·『화원악보』·『근화악부』·『가곡원류』·『여창가요록』·『남훈태평가』 등에 실려 전해진다.[30] 작품 속 남녀 중의 하나는 상대방을 짝사랑하고 있음이 분명

---

[30] 심재완,『교본 역대시조전서』, 773쪽 No. 2180[우리두리 後生ᄒ여 네 나되고 닉 너되야닉 너 그려 긋던 이를 너도 날 그려 긋쳐보렴平生에 닉 셜워ᄒ던 줄을 돌녀볼가 ᄒ노래] 참조.

하다. 짝사랑의 괴로움에 시달리던 일방(一方)이 상대방에 대한 원망
을 승화시켜 절절하게 내뱉고 있기 때문이다. 번역시를 다시 우리말
로 번역하면 다음과 같다.

> 우리 다음 생에 바뀌어 보세
> 그대는 내가 되고 나는 그대가 되어,
> 내가 내 평생 해온 것처럼
> 그대는 헛된 삶 속에서 나를 그리워하면
> 아마도 그대는 알게 될 걸?
> 나를 외롭게 지켜가며 내가 어떤 고통을 느꼈는지!
>
> 〈졸역〉

번역시가 원작 못지않게 아름다울 수 있는 것은 번역자와 원작자가
작품 구조 속에서 교감을 이룰 수 있었기 때문이다. 번역시의 첫 두
행은 원작의 초장과 완벽하게 일치한다. 원작 중장의 내용['내가 너를
그리워하여 끊던 애를 너도 나를 그리워하여 끊어보렴']을 번역자는 '내가
내 평생 해온 것처럼 너는 헛된 삶 속에서 나를 그리워하면'으로 바꿨
다. '애를 끊다'는 말을 영어로 번역하기 어렵기 때문이었겠지만, '애
끊듯 그리워 함'을 '헛된 삶 속에서 그리워 함'으로 바꾼 것은 번역자
의 탁월한 안목이었다. 종장['평생에 내 설워하던 줄을 돌려 볼까 하노라']
의 '돌려보다'는 '되돌려 주다'는 뜻과 '반대로 경험하다'는 뜻을 합친
개념이다. '내가 받은 괴로움'을 상대방에게 돌려주겠다는 뜻과 '그
괴로움을 너도 한 번 경험해보라'는 뜻이 합쳐져 있는 말이다. 그것을
번역자는 '나를 외롭게 지켜가며 내가 어떤 고통을 느꼈는지 경험해
보라'는 취지로 바꾸었다. 원작자의 의도를 포괄하면서도 원시에 비

해 훨씬 풍부한 시상을 보여줌으로써 성공적인 번역시로 만들어낸 사례다.

둘째, 번역자의 해석적 의도를 중시한 경우

의도했건 그렇지 않건, 번역시에는 어느 정도 번역자의 해석적 의도가 반영되기 마련이다. 해석이란 여러 가지 현상이나 혹은 그 언어에 의한 표현이 지니는 의미를 명확히 분석하여 논리화 시키는 것을 말한다. 물론 작품에 대한 감상자의 해석을 또 다른 작품으로 표현할 수도 있는데, 이 경우의 해석은 단순한 논리화를 뛰어넘는 창조적 행위다. '좋은 번역은 이미 문학작품에 대한 훌륭한 해석'[31]이라는 말도 따지고 보면 문학작품에 대한 번역은 해석을 전제로 하는 작업임을 나타낸다. 번역자 자신도 서문에서 이미 그런 고민을 말한 바 있다. 즉 시조에 종종 등장하는 '님'이란 단어는 많은 뜻을 함축하고 있기 때문에 그 뜻을 해석하기 위해 다양한 유추가 필요하다고 했다. 즉 '님'이란 말은 '내가 헌신하는 사람[즉 나를 소유하고 있는 사람]'이나 왕 또는 다른 헌신의 주체를 상징하는 경우도 많다고 했다. 그래서 번역자가 시조를 번역하는 데 이 단어의 혼돈을 없애기 위해 많은 노력을 기울였다는 것이다.

우선 앞에서 인용한 바 있는 황진이 노래의 번역시조[32]를 살펴보자. 이 번역시의 원작[33]은 유명한 기생 황진이가 왕실의 종친이었던

---

31 김지원, 앞의 논문, 71쪽.

32 앞 장 말미에 인용한 "You boisterous torrent, why so haste,~"를 말함.

33 심재완, 『교본 역대시조전서』, 1045쪽 No.2858[靑山裏 碧溪水야 수이 감을 즈랑마라 一到滄海ᄒ면 다시 오기 어려오니 明月이 滿空山ᄒ니 쉬여 간들 엇더리] 참조.

벽계수(碧溪守)란 사람과 명월(明月)[황진이 자신의 기명(妓名)]을 작품에 등장시켜 유혹의 의사를 표출한 것으로 알려진 노래다. 말하자면 중의적(重義的) 기법을 동원하여 작자의 뜻을 표명했다는 것인데, 이 점에 대하여 학계의 이론(異論)은 아직 없는 듯하다. 번역시를 우리말로 다시 번역하면 다음과 같다.

콸콸 흘러가는 급류야, 왜 그리 서두르느냐,
돌투성이 강바닥 위로 그렇게 달려들어
네 빠르기와 취미를 자랑하려느냐?
바다로 흘러 들어간 후엔 모든 게 끝이라네.
되돌릴 수 없나니. 그렇다면 왜 머물러,
달 빛 잠긴 언덕에 서성이며 노닐지 않느냐?

〈졸역〉

사실 원작에는 '벽계수'와 '명월'이 있어 해석의 단초로 작용한다. 두 소재 모두 자연물과 인간을 동시에 의미하는 중의적 개념들이기 때문에 노래 전체의 함의(含意)를 해석해내는 데 큰 어려움은 없다. 그러나 번역시의 경우는 완전한 자연의 묘사로 전환된 느낌이 있다. 번역자가 이 작품의 이중적 의미를 전제로 했다면, 좀 더 용어를 교묘하게 다루었어야 했다고 본다. 번역시의 핵심은 'torrent'와 'stay, linger by moonlit hills and play'에 있다. 'torrent'가 모종의 심리학적 내포를 지녔다거나 'stay/linger/play/moonlit hills' 등이 어떤 메타포적 표현들인지 알 수는 없으나, 'torrent'에 인격적 의미를 부여한 것만 제외한다면, '남녀 간 감정의 움직임'을 상정한 원작과 판이하게 달라졌음을 부정할 수 없다. '남성에 대한 여성의 유혹'이라는 원작의 의도가 '자연의 움직임에 대한 의인화(擬人化)'로 재해석된 모습을 쉽게 발견할 수 있다는 것이다. 말하자면 '원작[자연의 묘사→ 남녀 간 애정사]➡번역시[남녀 간 애정사→자연의 묘사]'로의 전환은 결국 번역시의 본질을 '자연의 묘사'로 귀결시킨 것이니, 번역을 통한 원작의 재해석으로 이해할 수밖에 없을 것이다.

해석적 견해를 반영한 또 다른 번역시조를 살펴보기로 한다.

> Dream for me far-away love brought
>
> As good as dead to wakeful hope.
>
> I, passion-mad, like one distraught,
>
> Awoke and scanned all in my scope.
>
> Lo! she was gone, fair child of May,
>
> As if, she, pigued, had fled away.
>
> 〈I-jung-sin〉

이 작품은 영조 때 가객이었던 이정신(李廷藎)의 시조를 번역한 것이다. 원작[34]은 꿈속에서 만난 님이 꿈 깬 후에 종적 없이 사라졌다는 탄식의 노래다. 번역시를 우리말로 바꾸면 다음과 같다.

> 꿈은 내게 먼 곳의 사랑을 데려왔고
>
> 죽은 것과 같던 나를 희망으로 깨웠네
>
> 정열에 미친 난, 흥분으로 제 정신 아닌 것처럼
>
> 깨어나 주변의 모든 것을 뒤졌네

---

34 심재완, 『교본 역대시조전서』, 120쪽, No.343[꿈이 날 爲ᄒ야 먼듸 님 ᄃ려와늘 탐탐이 반기너겨 줌ᄭᆡ야 니러보니 그 님이 怒ᄒ여 간지 긔도망도 업세라] 참조.

아! 그녀는 갔다네, 오월의 착한 아이는

마치, 날아간 것처럼 그녀는 사라졌다네.

〈졸역〉

　원작의 '님'은 분명 사랑하는 이성이다. 꿈속에서나 만날 수 있는 님이라면 살아있는 님이 아니거나, 살아 있어도 짝사랑하는 님일 것이다. 꿈속에 찾아온 님을 현실로 착각하고 일어나 보니 '노하여 가버렸는지' 그 님은 그 자리에 없더라는 것이다. 원작시에는 이처럼 두 가지의 모호함이 들어 있다. 번역자가 그 님을 짝사랑의 대상으로 보았는가 사별한 님으로 보았는가에 따라 번역시도 달라져야 할 것이다. 그런데 번역시는 자못 서사적이어서 복잡하다. 그 서사 내용[꿈속에서 먼 곳의 사랑하는 사람을 만났다/그동안 (절망으로) 죽은 것처럼 지내던 내게 꿈속에서나마 갑자기 희망을 주었다/꿈에서 깨어난 나는 정열과 흥분으로 어쩔 줄 모르며 주변을 샅샅이 뒤졌다/그러나 그녀는 날아간 것처럼 사라졌다]은 간략한 원작에 비해 매우 화려하며 수사적이다. 시적 자아인 나는 얼마 전까지 가까이에 사는 한 여인을 사모해왔을 것이다. 그런데 부모의 강압에 못 이겨 그녀는 먼 곳으로 시집을 가버렸다. 그래서 시적 자아는 '죽은 것처럼' 절망의 시간을 보내고 있었다. 그런데 문득 꿈에서 그녀가 찾아왔고, 절망에 젖어있던 나는 갑작스런 희망의 상황을 맞게 되었다. 그러나 꿈을 깨고 현실로 돌아오니 그녀는 '새가 날아간 것처럼' 그 자리에 없었고, 그 빈자리를 절망이 대신하고 있다는, 잿빛 분위기의 노래다.

　사실 원작에서 노래되고 있는 단순한 꿈 이야기를 자기 식으로 해석하여 하나의 스토리로 완성해내는 것이 쉬운 일은 아니다. 더구나 그 대상을 서구식으로 윤색해내기란 더더욱 어려운 일이다. 그런데 그는 그녀를 'fairchild of May'라 명명했다. 비록 짝사랑이긴 하나 시적 자아인 내가 얼마나 그녀를 갈망하는지를 이 단어들은 보여준다. 이 번역이 번역자의 해석적 견해를 바탕으로 하고 있다는 점도 그런 점에서 타당하다.

나가는 말

지금까지 변영태의 영역시조를 대상으로 그 성격과 의미를 살펴보았다. 그는 우탁(禹倬), 정몽주(鄭夢周) 등 유명씨 55명과 무명씨들의 작품 총 102편을 골라 번역했다. 그가 선정한 작자들은 양반 사대부, 중인, 기녀 등으로 분류되는데, 기녀를 제외한 나머지 작자들은 대개 현실정치에 참여하던 뛰어난 문인, 학자, 무인, 가객 등 비교적 모든 계층에 골고루 분포되어 있음을 확인하게 된다. 작품의 주제 역시 탄노(歎老), 충절(忠節), 교훈(敎訓), 회고(懷古), 신념(信念), 우국(憂國), 자적(自適), 안빈(安貧), 번민(煩悶), 연모(戀慕), 자연친화(自然親和), 허무(虛無), 취락(醉樂)[혹은 향락(享樂)], 풍자(諷刺), 효친(孝親), 한거(閑居), 망향(望鄕), 흥(興), 자탄(自歎), 원망(怨望) 등으로 다양하다.대개 낭만시의 범주에 속하는 옛 시조의 본질을 벗어나 주제적 측면에서 현실과 낭만을 적절히 조화시키려는 번역자의 의도가 강하게 작용한 것으로 보인다. 즉 현실과 꿈을 바탕으로 삶의 전반적인 면을 보여주고자 한 것이 번역자의 의도였던 것이다.

변영태가 무엇보다 시조의 본질을 정확히 인식하고 있었다는 점은 번역자로서의 가장 큰 장점이었다. 시조가 중국 시와 구별되는 반면 영국의 소네트와 유사한 규칙성을 갖고 있었다고 본 점은 자신이 시도한 시조 영역 작업의 당위성을 강조하려 했거나, 시조가 '중국 시와 구별되는 오랜 전통을 가진 순수 한국어로 된 시가'임을 강조함으로써 근대 이전에 성행했던 시조의 한역이 시조의 본질상 그다지 탐탁한 일은 아니었음과 시조의 영역이 시대정신에 맞는 일임을 암시하려는 뜻이었을 것이다. 시조를 '본질적으로 노래 부르기 위한 장르'로 본 그의 관점은 시조부흥론 시기를 포함하여 당시까지 지식인으로서 '시조가 노래'라는 인식을 갖기란 쉽지 않은 일이었음을 감안할 때 탁월한 관점이었다. 시조부흥운동을 거치면서 지식사회에 고착된 오해들 가운데 하나는 '시조가 우리 고유의 시'라는 편견이었다. 전통 시조를 시형의 하나로만 인식하려고 했던 당시 지식인들과 달리 변영태는 시조가 노래라는 인식을 갖고 있었기 때문에 옛 시조의 내용이 심오하지 않다는 점에 대하여 크게 개의하지 않았다. 시조는 하나의 유흥적 표현수단이었을 뿐 사상과 철학을 담은 담론체계는 아니었다는 것이다. 변영태가 영어 번역에의 의욕을 가질 수 있었던 것도 그가 시조의 본질, 특히 언어적 짜임의 규칙성이나 시정신이 한시보다는 영시와 통한다고 본 점 때문이었으리라 생각한다.

사실 원작자의 의도를 100% 재현하는 것은 불가능하지만, 변영태의 영역 시조들 가운데 가장 큰 비중을 차지하는 것이 원작자의 의도를 재현한 경우다. 직역·의역·모방 등 번역의 세 유형들 가운데 가장 바람직한 것이 의역이라 한다면, 그것은 원작자의 정신적·문화적 배경을 숙지해야 하고, 양쪽의 언어에 능통해야 함을 의미한다. 변영태의 영역시 가운데 이 범주에 속한 대부분의 작품들은 번역자가 원작의 이면적 의미까지 분명히 통찰한 다음 그것을 영미권의 독자들이 알기 쉽도록 그 쪽 개념으로 바꾸거나 풀어 놓는 방법을 씀으로써 무리 없는 번역이 될 수 있었다.

번역자의 해석적 의도가 반영된 번역 작품들의 경우도 원작자의 의도를 최대한 재현한 경우들과 전혀 다르다고 할 수는 없다. 번역시에는 원작에 대한 번역자의 해석적 의도가 반영되기 마련이라는 점, 여러 가지 현상이나 표현이 지니는 의미를 명확히 분석하여 논리화 시키는 것이야말로 해석 행위의 핵심이라는 점 등을 감안하면 사실 모든 번역이 해석일 수 있는 것이다. '좋은 번역은 이미 문학작품에 대한 훌륭한 해석'이라는 말도 번역자는 특별한 의도 없이 좋은 해석자가 되어야 함을 뜻한다. 이 점에서 변영태의 시조 영역은 원작의 의미를 서구식으로 충실하게 해석한 결과였다고 할 수 있다.

본격적인 시조 영역의 선례들이 없는 상황에서 스스로 시조의 본질에 대한 탐구를 바탕으로 영역을 시도함으로써 후대 인사들에게 시조 영역의 모범을 보인 점에 변영태의 장점이 있다. 그의 시조 영역은 그 분야의 첫 사례라는 점과 함께 좋은 번역의 출발이었다는 점을 인정할만한 요인들을 적지 않게 지니고 있으며, 요즈음 고창하는 한국문학의 세계화를 당시에 이미 실천했다는 점에서도 매우 선구적인 작업이었다고 할 수 있다.

*이 글은 《溫知論叢》 29호[2011. 9. 30.]에 실린 필자의 논문
"변영태 英譯時調의 특징과 의미"를 약간 고친 내용임.

저자 | 변영태

정치가, 영문학자, 호는 일석(逸石).

고려대학교 교수, UN한국수석대표, 외무부장관, 국무총리 역임.

주요저서로, 〈나의 조국〉, 〈외교어록〉, 〈Tales From Korea〉 등이 있음.

편자 | 민충환

문학평론가, 부천대 명예교수.

주요저서로, 〈이태준 연구〉, 〈이문구 소설어 사전〉 외에

책임편집으로 〈계용묵전집〉, 〈한흑구문학선집〉, 〈현덕소설집〉 등이 있음.

SONGS FROM KOREA_변영태가 쓴 영시집

초판 인쇄 | 2011년 10월 19일
초판 발행 | 2011년 10월 28일

저 자 변영태
편 자 민충환

책임편집 윤예미

발 행 처 도서출판 지식과교양
등록번호 제 2010-19호
주 소 서울시 도봉구 창5동 320번지 행정지원센터 B104
전 화 (02) 900-4520 (대표)/ 편집부 (02) 900-4521
팩 스 (02) 900-1541
전자우편 kncbook@hanmail.net

ⓒ 변영태 2011 All rights reserved. Printed in KOREA

ISBN 978-89-94955-46-9 03810   **정가** 22,000원